TIDES OF WAR

BOOK FOUR
ENDURANCE

C. Alexander London

SCHOLASTIC INC.

ISBN 978-0-545-80081-5

10 9 8 7 6 5 4 3 2 1   15 16 17 18 19

Printed in the U.S.A.   40
First printing 2015

Book design by Sharismar Rodriguez & Carol Ly

To my teachers and to yours

PROLOGUE

CRACKS ran like canyons through the ice sheet atop the Arctic Ocean, some of them narrow enough for a man to hop across on foot, some of them wider than the Mississippi River. I peered down through the helicopter window, wondering what the ocean below the ice had in store for me.

For us.

I was not going in alone. I had a partner with me.

Even with my wraparound sunglasses on, the glare of the sun off the ice was blinding. The Arctic Ocean was a barren landscape, frozen solid — although not as frozen this spring as it used to be. Every year, the ice broke up a little earlier, shrank back a little farther, melted faster, and cracked deeper and deeper.

Those cracks were the reason my team and I had come so far north, to the top of the world, nearly to the North Pole. We weren't up there looking for Santa Claus.

We were up there looking for trouble.

The United States Navy had sent me and my partner with a small support team to meet up with the Research Vessel *Buzz Aldrin*, whose crew was studying the ocean floor and the ice floes of the Arctic Circle, mapping the new shipping lanes opened up by melting ice and exploring for oil.

The ship had recently lost some valuable and sensitive research equipment, and it seemed their best chance of finding it was the furry, fish-breathed sea lion in the crate next to me. Let's call him Hansel, like the fairy-tale kid who left a trail of bread crumbs through the forest to find his way home. That's not the sea lion's real name, though. His identity has become a military secret, and I don't think I should go writing it down. I'm already risking a lot telling this story.

You see, I'm a Marine Mammal handler for the United States Navy, and officially, my mission with Hansel on the Arctic ice sheet never happened. The navy would deny it if they were asked about it, and so would I. That was the deal I made after everything that happened up there: I would keep my mouth shut, and the navy would deny everything, and things could go on like normal in the Arctic Circle. The hunt for oil would continue, and so would the competition among scientists and politicians from five different countries to claim as much territory as they could while the ice melted. Submarines would still skulk below the surface, and oil platforms would drill on isolated seas, and the research vessels would plod along, making maps, planting flags, and acting as if they'd always belonged up there at the top of the world.

No one would ever mention the people who died on my mission or the animal who was in the crate beside me on that helicopter flying in. As far as the United States Navy is concerned, this mission and this sea lion never existed.

But he did exist.

He was my partner.

And even though I shouldn't say a word, I'm going to tell you what happened to him.

I owe that sea lion my life. The least I can do is tell his story.

01:
SIR, NO, SIR

OUR helicopter flew over the edge of the great expanse of Arctic ice and came in low across the blue-green water of the Chukchi Sea.

"Fifteen minutes, sir," the crew chief told me through the intercom in my headset. We wouldn't be able to hear each other at all over the roar of the rotor blades and the wind if it weren't for the intercom, and even then I had trouble hearing him. Had he just called me *sir*?

"I'm not an officer," I told him.

"What's that, sir?"

"I said I'm not an officer," I repeated over the static of the mic. "You don't need to call me *sir*."

The crew chief gave me a funny look, like why would I object to being called *sir*. It was just one of those things that civilians usually didn't understand. The whole crew of the helicopter was made up of civilians and so was the crew of the ship we were heading to. Only two other members of my team were in the military, and none of us were officers. Officers were the managers and bosses, and even the most senior enlisted sailor had to call even the youngest, most inexperienced officer *sir*.

It was amazing how well those three letters could be used by a salty sea-dog enlisted man to call some young lieutenant a moron without the officer ever realizing it. Like "Yes, *sir*, the water is very blue today, *sir*," or "No, *sir*, I don't think it's a good idea to juggle with live hand grenades, *sir*."

I wasn't much of a fan of officers.

I'd joined the navy right out of high school and worked my way up the ranks of enlisted personnel over the last few years to become a petty officer second class, rated as a Marine Mammal Systems operator, which meant I helped train, handle, care for, and document the work of the navy's dolphins and sea lions. I was proud of the hard work it had taken to become one of the best handlers in the navy's arsenal, so I didn't want this helicopter crewman from the Research Vessel *Buzz Aldrin* thinking I was some paper-pushing *officer*. I worked for a living.

But instead of telling him all that over the static of the intercom and the whomp of the helicopter blades, I just gave him a smile and turned back to my sea lion in his crate.

"Hansel" was chocolate brown, with big black eyes as wide as a cow's. He had little nubs for ears — which is why sea lions are also known as "eared seals" — and long, twitching whiskers at the end of his pointy snout. His snout also had a patch of tan fur right on the end, which I thought made him look dignified, an illusion that he always undid by hopping back and forth on his front flippers and barking whenever I paid him any attention. He was, in truth, more like an eager puppy than a majestic creature of the sea — a seven-hundred-pound puppy with a bone-crushing bite. He was also an expert at playing fetch.

With my guidance, Hansel had recovered torpedoes dropped on the ocean floor during training exercises, the lost "black box" recording device from a crashed airplane's cockpit five hundred feet below the ocean's surface, and an admiral's cell phone, which he had dropped off the side of a navy destroyer while yelling at some unfortunate junior officer.

Now we'd been sent to the Arctic Circle to fetch some expensive research equipment that had fallen through a crack in the ice sheet. I didn't know a lot about the mission yet, just that the civilian research ship had requested us, that they were funded by the navy, and that the mission had some kind of strategic importance to the United States.

"The Russian military is operating in the area," my commander had told me before I left Naval Base Point Loma in San Diego. "But we do not expect any inter-ference from them. They've got their own oil and natural gas operations up there, and as long as we don't get in their way, they won't get in ours. Your primary dangers are going to be the cold — the water up there is far colder than what our sea lions are used to — and natural predators. Orcas feed off the local seal and wal-rus population, and this time of year, the polar bears are actively hunting. They eat seals and sea lions, too. You'll have to remain alert."

"Aye aye, *sir*," I told the commander, jabbing that *sir* in like a blade. As if I didn't know that the Arctic was cold or that killer whales and polar bears ate sea lions. I'd been working with Hansel for almost two years and read all the research about sea lions that I could get my hands on. I also had a subscription to

National Geographic. Just because I didn't have a college degree didn't mean I was a dummy.

In the cargo helicopter with me, I had the pieces to construct a large onboard cage for Hansel, a special warming vest the navy had invented for cold-water operations, and enough restaurant-quality fish to last my sea lion a week. I had all the equipment I'd need for the operation, and enough medical supplies to treat Hansel for anything from the sniffles to a heart attack.

I also had Dr. Morris, a civilian veterinarian who'd been with the program for ages, to actually provide Hansel's medical care, and two Marine Mammal technicians. Together, my people, my sea lion, the equipment, and I made up what we called the MK 5 System — "QuickFind" for short. We traveled with everything we needed, and we were prepared for anything the Arctic could throw at us.

At least, that's what I thought.

Until everything went wrong.

02:
COUNTRY OF THE BEAR

WHEN we set down on the deck of the *Buzz Aldrin* and began to off-load our gear, I was all confidence.

The captain came out to greet us and had his crew assist us double-time to off-load and set up our equipment belowdecks.

"We need to get the chopper out of here fast," he explained to me. "A storm's coming in and we don't have a hangar on board to protect it. I'm not going to be held responsible for ruining a thirty-million-dollar navy helicopter."

"Yes, sir," I told him, and he cocked his head at me.

"No need to call me *sir*, son," he replied. "I work for a living."

I couldn't help but laugh. I liked the captain already.

"Captain Carl Peterson of the National Arctic Research Institute at your service," he introduced himself.

"Navy Marine Mammal Handler Second Class Ryan Keene." I stuck my hand out for a shake. "And this is Hansel."

I opened Hansel's crate and my sea lion bounced out on his front flippers, his massive neck heaving him forward. He stopped in front of Captain Peterson, settled back on his haunches, and lifted one flipper into the air. He let out a sharp bark, and Captain Peterson flinched.

"It's okay, Captain," I said. "He wants a handshake, too."

The captain laughed and reached down to shake

my sea lion's front fin. Once the handshake was done, the sea lion saluted.

"Sorry about that," I said. "He can't help but salute a captain, officer or not."

"He's a navy man," the captain said. "I understand."

I patted Hansel on the head, and he made a low rumble that was almost like a cat purring.

"We'll motor into a protected bay for the night to ride out the storm," the captain told me. "And tomorrow we'll head for the recovery site. You'll need to cross some heavy ice to get there, but my team and I will take you. We really appreciate the navy sending you out here so fast."

"We go where we're needed," I told him. "Hansel here is about the best QuickFind sea lion we've got. And since the institute gets most of its funding from the navy, it's kind of our equipment that got lost anyway."

The captain laughed at that. We lived in different worlds, but we sort of worked for the same people.

"That's true," he said. "And it's some sensitive equipment. A whole drill and soil-analysis rig. Not sure how it broke free, but it's somewhere on the sea-floor deeper than we can go to get it. The data on its hard drive could be worth a fortune, and we'd prefer to get it back."

"Well, Captain," I told him, "I don't know much about drilling and soil analysis, but Hansel and I always find what we're after. I've worked with this furry guy for almost two years now, and I promise you, what you've lost won't stay lost for long." I handed him a copy of the QuickFind Services Request he had submitted to the navy, which had all the details for the size, shape, and location of the equipment he needed recovered. He looked it over and nodded.

"That's all correct," he told me. "Although there's one thing I didn't put in that form when I submitted it. There's another team nearby doing their own research. They've got their own equipment on the sea-floor, and they get pretty testy when our people get too near it."

"Testy?"

"They fired a warning shot our way one time," the captain said.

"A warning shot? Who are they?"

"They work for a private oil company," the captain said. "But they won't say which one and I can't seem to find out. Not even sure which country they're from, except I know it's not ours. Lord knows I've reported the incident to my superiors and gotten no answers. I thought you should know, because before you get to work, I set up a meeting with them for you."

"You set up a meeting for me?" Civilian captains didn't go setting up meetings between navy sailors and shady research teams from foreign companies. My jaw must have hit the deck while my eyebrows reached for the sky, because the captain knew immediately that he had some explaining to do.

"I had to introduce you," he said. "If they saw you guys out there without knowing who you were, I worried they'd start shooting again. And I imagine firing at a navy team like yours might turn into a bigger problem fast. No one wants a shoot-out on the Arctic Ocean, son. There are at least five different countries trying to control this region, and if one starts shooting, they'll all start shooting. I figured a meeting was the best way to avoid any trouble. It's a fragile peace up here, and we do our best to keep it, in our own way."

"It's your ship and your mission, Captain," I told him. "Hansel and I will do whatever you need."

"Thank you, sailor," the captain said, then left me and Hansel to get settled while he went back to the bridge of his ship.

"Strange mission, huh, fella?" I asked Hansel. He shook out his fur and sniffed at the air, completely indifferent to my doubts. He shivered, and I figured he noticed the air was a lot colder than it was down in Southern California.

"Yo, Bryson!" I called out to one of my technicians, Seaman Nate Bryson, an eager-eyed nineteen-year-old from Nebraska who'd never even seen the ocean before enlisting in the navy. Now he found himself nearly at the North Pole, gazing out into the frozen sea. "Stop sightseeing and get me Hansel's vest from that bin over there."

Bryson snapped to it, nearly tripping over himself to pull the waterproof fleece vest from a big plastic bin of sea lion gear.

The vest had a blue pixelated camo pattern on it to blend in with an aquatic environment in case he needed to be stealthy, and it was lined with a layer of lightweight Kevlar, to protect him from bites and from bullets — although in all our deployments, we'd never been attacked by anything or shot at by anyone. Still, the navy took the safety of its mammals seriously, and this vest was custom-made just for Hansel, to keep him protected and to keep him warm.

The moment I had it in my hands, Hansel barked excitedly. He'd practiced wearing it in an air-conditioned trailer a dozen times and on the deck of our small motorboat, but I'd never before put it on him because he needed it. This was Arctic survival gear. He let me slide it right over his head, and I tucked his flippers through the arm holes and fastened the heavy plastic buckle on the front. I hoped we didn't run into any of the local seals. I figured poor Hansel would be embarrassed. Then again, Hansel had spent his whole life around humans; maybe he thought of himself as one of us and didn't mind being dressed up. Or maybe sea lions didn't think of themselves as anything at all, and the embarrassment was all mine. Sea lions couldn't be embarrassed. That was purely a human emotion.

"Give him a hat and he'd look like a real sailor," Bryson joked.

"It's not a costume," I snapped at him. "And if you tried to put a funny hat on Hansel, he'd bite your hand off. I know from experience."

Bryson blushed and started to apologize, until I burst out laughing to show him I was kidding. I'd never actually tried to put a hat on my sea lion. Though I bet Hansel really would've bitten my hand off if I had.

"It's amazing, isn't it?" Bryson asked me as he turned to see our chopper get the all clear and lift off from the deck.

"The helicopter?" I asked.

"No." He pointed past the helicopter to the sea and the jagged white ice rising into the bright blank of the sky. "That."

It was the first time since landing I'd really looked around at our area of operations. Loose icebergs bobbed like desolate islands, their peaks above the water, vast mountains of ice below. On the horizon, the polar ice sheet began, a white cliff face that marked the beginning of the top of the world. Water flowed through open seams and breaks in its surface, and wind whipped dancing gusts of ice into a fine mist in the cold air.

Far off, the silhouette of a single polar bear plodded along the ice, its white fur barely visible against the snow, like a ghost stalking through the fog.

The Arctic got its name from the constellation of stars that the Greeks saw above the far North every night: *Ursa Major*, the Great Bear. The ancient Greek word for bear was *arktos*, and they called the whole region of earth below the bear-shaped constellation *arktikos*, meaning "of the bear."

The Greeks had never seen a polar bear and probably didn't know of their existence. They hadn't named this region after the polar bear. They'd named it after the giant bear in the sky, a bear made of stars. But looking at the solitary white bear on the ice, perfectly adapted to its frozen environment, I knew the Greeks had named the place right. We were in his country; the country of the polar bear.

I had hoped to see one in the wild, and now, almost as soon as I'd arrived, I'd seen one. I felt amazingly lucky.

"Yeah," I told Bryson. "This really is beautiful."

At the time, I had no idea how deadly such a beautiful place could be, nor how unlucky I actually was, but I was going to find all that out very, very soon.

Polar bears weren't the only danger awaiting us on the ice.

03:
ROLLING IN THE DEEP

THAT night, on the top rack in our berth deep in the ship's hull, I lay awake thinking about the day ahead. Well, actually, I lay awake trying to take deep breaths and not throw up as our ship rolled and heaved in the stormy Chukchi Sea.

My body was tossed against the wall one moment, the next it was thrown against the netting that was strung up to prevent a sleeper from falling out of bed in a storm just like this one. In the rack below me, Bryson snored loudly. Since I was awake anyway and unlikely to fall asleep anytime soon, I figured I might as well think through the next day's work.

I'd studied the paperwork that the *Buzz Aldrin* had submitted to request a navy sea lion QuickFind team. It detailed the equipment they had lost to a crack in the ice. Even though I didn't understand exactly what all the equipment did, I knew the size and shape of the lost drill bits and sample collection bins and motorized soil-analysis robots. We'd made models of them all back in San Diego and spent several weeks training Hansel to find them in the dark ocean.

It gave me a kind of comfort to know that when scientists lost a robot, they needed a living animal like Hansel to help them find it. Maybe all those science fiction movies were wrong: Robots weren't going to take over the world. They couldn't even keep from getting lost in the ocean.

It was pretty simple how the QuickFind System worked. I'd trained Hansel to respond to a set of commands and gestures by rewarding him with fish and toys. To get those rewards, he had to find the object I wanted in response to each unique gesture and instruction. He would attach a clamp that he carried in his mouth to the item, tug on the line attached to the clamp to make sure it was secure, then return to me while I reeled the object in. If the wrong thing came up, I simply ignored the mistake, gave him back the clamp, and repeated the order. When he attached it to the correct object, then he got his reward. He was pretty eager for snacks, so he learned fairly quickly which command related to which object and which of the other trick objects I'd scattered about he could ignore. No sense having him haul up half the seafloor.

I was excited to show Captain Peterson and his team what the navy's Marine Mammal Systems could do. I pressed the light on my watch to check the time. It was only one in the morning. There was a lot of night left ahead, and a lot of storm left to get through. I was glad I'd skipped dinner. It hadn't looked that good coming out of the ship's galley, and it definitely wouldn't have looked good coming back out of me.

I got up to visit Hansel in the cargo hold where we'd set up his big pen, with a pool of water to splash in and plenty of room to move around. Our other technician, Kincaid, was on duty, making sure Hansel didn't get hurt with the swaying of the ship or feel stressed and lonely in an unfamiliar place.

"How's he doing?" I asked her.

"Sound asleep," she said without looking up from the novel she was reading, one of the futuristic Teenagers vs. the System books that they were always making movies of. "Listen to him snoring."

I listened, and beneath the roar of the engines and the howl of the wind off the ocean, I heard the slow, steady grumbling snores of my sea lion. His face twitched in his sleep, making his whiskers dance up and down. I had no idea what sea lions dreamed about, but the way he was wiggling and snoring and grunting, I was pretty sure it was a good dream. Probably out hunting fish in the wild. Or did he dream of himself in a sailor's uniform, walking and talking like a person? He'd spent far more time with people than wild sea lions; maybe he even dreamed like a person.

The ship made a sudden heave as it plummeted into the trench of a large wave and then slammed up and out the other side of it. I nearly lost my footing, and poor Hansel, sound asleep, rolled like a sausage in a pan to the edge of his pen. The sudden movement woke him, and he popped onto his fins in surprise. His eyes met mine in what I could swear was a "what gives?" sort of look.

"I think it's time we secure him," Kincaid suggested. If I'd been on duty all night, it would have been done hours ago, but this was her first at-sea deployment with the program and I guess the seas hadn't been quite so rough before that moment.

We both moved to Hansel's enclosure. Kincaid opened the door, and I made the motion for Hansel to climb into his padded hammock.

Hansel lurched across the pen with a gleeful bark and heaved himself into the heavy-duty canvas hammock. It was padded and lined with fleece, hung within reach of a water dispenser so he could drink if he got thirsty, but it had straps across the top to keep him secure inside it, not unlike the netted bunks for humans. I snapped the straps shut and rubbed his head, which he answered with another joyous bark.

"Get some rest, pal," I told him. "We've got to show off for these civilians tomorrow. Show 'em what a navy marine mammal can do."

He nuzzled his snout against my palm, then settled in back to sleep. I climbed back out of his pen and shut the door.

"You should get some rest, too," Kincaid told me. "You've got a long day tomorrow."

"I'm too on edge to sleep," I told her. "I always get this way before a mission. Even training."

"They told me you were a perfectionist," she said.

"Who did?"

"The other handlers back in San Diego," she answered. "They warned me that you like your sea lion more than you like most people."

"My sea lion smells better than most people," I joked.

We both knew that wasn't true. Hansel had his charms but he smelled terrible, a mixture of dead fish, sour vegetables, wet fur, and salt water.

Joking like that was a habit I had, covering up uncomfortable truths with sarcasm. I'd done it ever since middle school. I guess people really did make me kind of uncomfortable. I never knew what they were thinking. Sometimes their actions and words didn't match, or their smiles said one thing but their words another.

A sea lion's thoughts were far more mysterious than a person's, but also didn't matter as much. A sea lion couldn't lie or hide his reasons for doing something. Sea lions didn't have a way to be dishonest. You could trust them, as long as you were careful not to forget that they were powerful animals. They had muscle and teeth and instincts, and they didn't get sentimental. I liked the simplicity of my relationship to them.

Relationships with people weren't simple at all. So I made jokes. It was a defense.

Kincaid didn't really laugh, though. She kind of just shrugged and went back to her seat to fill out a form that described the ship's roll and Hansel's roll with it and what time we put him in his hammock. In the Marine Mammal Program, everything that happened had to be written down in a report. We all probably spent as much time doing paperwork as we did working with animals. Maybe more.

Kincaid had been right. I had a mission to do the next day and I'd have the paperwork to do afterward, and I needed to sleep. Come sunup, we'd be trekking inland on the Arctic ice sheet and I'd be responsible for Hansel's success and his safety in a new environment. I'd need my wits about me.

But I wasn't ready to say good night yet. I don't remember how long I stood there outside Hansel's enclosure, watching his chest rise and fall as he breathed, but even after I went back to my rack to sleep, I could still hear the sea lion's deep rumbling snores in my dreams.

Or maybe that was Bryson snoring. In their sleep, navy men and navy sea lions sounded a lot alike. Sadly, as a deep breath through my nose made clear to me, they smelled alike, too. I was doubly glad I'd skipped dinner.

04:
THE WILD NORTH

THE R/V *Buzz Aldrin* docked directly against the ice
the next morning in calm and crystal clear water.
The crew dropped long metal ramps from the fore-
deck onto the thick frozen surface. Two transport
vehicles waited to drive us across the polar region to
the inland station where the other research team was
based.

In the distance, a vast ice sheet rose from the emer-
ald ocean like a sheer cliff made of marble. The wind
blew ice from its flat surface, forming a fragile rainbow
in the hazy mist. Against the backdrop of white ice

and white snow and white sky, the colors seemed more vibrant than any I'd ever seen.

I turned inland, and saw our transport vehicles, which were hulking bright orange blocks, like tractors set on top of rolling tank treads that gave them the ability to move across a variety of terrain. The sea ice could be rough, with huge crevasses and massive boulders of ice that were spit out as large ice sheets — or floes, as they were sometimes called — crashed into each other. The seams where two floes met could be small lines of rough ice strewn with boulders no higher than a man's knees or giant pressure ridges, rising one or two stories tall. And since the floes were always moving, the terrain up here was always changing. So the vehicles really had to be *all-terrain*.

One of the vehicles had a flatbed trailer attached, which was where Hansel and his crate would ride, along with our team's supply of clamps and pulleys and lines. The trailer was otherwise empty, though, because on the way back it would be filled with the equipment we recovered.

The rest of the gear was loaded into the storage bays below the cabin of each vehicle, like the luggage area under a bus. There were heat blankets and solar stoves and ice axes and ropes and emergency medical packs. They even had dynamite and remote detonators in case we had to blast through an extremely tall pressure ridge. I didn't know what else the crew of the *Buzz Aldrin* had brought along, but I trusted the captain to provide for the humans' needs, while I provided for the sea lion's.

"Let's hope we don't need that stuff," Dr. Morris, the veterinarian, said. "I'd prefer to be bored on this deployment."

"They've got a medic for us," I told her. "You only get busy if Hansel's in trouble . . . and that is not gonna happen on my watch."

"Good to hear it," she said. "But nature can be

unforgiving and unpredictable. I wouldn't get too cocky about it."

"We're prepared," I said, immediately regretting how arrogant I sounded. I couldn't help it. If I wasn't making a sarcastic comment, I was making an over-confident one. Dr. Morris just raised her eyebrows at me and climbed up into the cabin of the first vehicle.

While the rest of my team climbed on board after the veterinarian, I volunteered to ride on the trailer with Hansel to make sure he stayed comfortable. He had on his polar vest, but I still worried it might be too cold for him in the open air. In truth, I also didn't particularly want to climb into another steel can for our three-hour drive across the Arctic. The previous night's fitful sleep was enough time cooped up inside for me. I preferred to be outside. I had on a big parka and hat and boots, and I had a wrap around my neck that I could pull up for a face mask if I needed to. I was about as prepared for the cold as I could be. And I was looking forward to the view. How often did a person get to ride around on an open trailer at the top of the world?

Once Captain Peterson and his people had climbed into their vehicle, the drivers radioed to each other and the two big transports rolled out in single file with a roar of their engines and a belch of black smoke. We were on our way north.

"Ever think you'd ride in a trailer across the Arctic, Hansel?" I asked. Even with the loud engines, I knew Hansel could hear my voice. Sea lions have amazing hearing, which helps them above and below the water. He'd have no idea what I was saying, of course, but I thought the sound of my voice might comfort him in what was probably a strange and confusing moment for the poor guy. It was a strange and confusing moment for me, too, but I felt glad for the navy at that moment, grateful for the chance they'd given me to do what I loved in such a beautiful place.

It was early spring, so the ice had just begun to melt, forming scattered ponds and pools along the surface.

Each pond reflected the pearl-white sky back at itself. The water shined and shimmered, small ripples vibrating the surface when we rumbled by. Each pond looked like a portal to another world. There were rough patches where ice had shifted, thin areas of dangerous gray ice that couldn't hold the weight of the trucks, and crazy pressure ridges that looked like ocean waves that had frozen at their peaks, forming crystal statues of the moment before they crashed. The sight reminded me that we were actually driving on ice on top of an ocean.

A few yards ahead, a spurt of mist rose up from the ice. I pulled out my binoculars to look at that spot and saw there was a small dip in the surface. As we drove past, I kept my view fixed on the spot, and a few minutes later, another spurt of mist erupted from it. It was, I realized, a breathing hole cut into the ice from underneath.

During the winter, when the whole area is frozen solid, ringed seals spend most of their time underwater. But they're mammals, just like Hansel, and they need to come up for air to breathe. Because the ice sheet is so vast, they could easily drown before finding open water, so they've developed a way to use their snouts and the claws on their flippers to dig breathing holes at various spots along the ice sheet. Seeing one in action, I was amazed not just at how the animals managed to make these holes, but also that they could remember where they were in the vastness of the ocean.

Knowing as we drove that there was a sea just a few feet below us, where seals, walruses, and killer whales swam and hunted, where the depths and trenches had not even been mapped, gave me a feeling I can only describe as uncanny.

The ground felt both solid and timeless, but it was neither of those things. It was several feet thick, but it was ever changing, shifting, and drifting on the currents.

Now that spring had begun, it was also melting.

It melted a little every year, opening the ocean up, and refroze every winter, but from what I'd read, the ice up here was melting earlier and faster than at any time in recorded history. The Arctic winters had become shorter and warmer, and in the spring and summer months, new channels were opened in the ice, allowing more ships through than ever before . . . and giving access to more of the oil and natural gas below the ocean floor. The energy-hungry nations of the world were in a race to see who would control this region's future, who would have access to the new shipping lanes, and who could profit from the huge reserves of undersea fossil fuels. The Russian military had deployed ships and planes and helicopters to the region, while the Danish, Finnish, Canadian, and Norwegian governments had all sent research and military vessels to secure their own claims. The United States had, too, although the politicians in Washington were moving much more slowly than those of some of the other governments.

The US Navy owned the *Buzz Aldrin*, but the ship was operated by a civilian research team from the

National Arctic Research Institute, as were two other American vessels in the region. The institute was run by civilians, but its board of directors had several admirals and generals on it, so it was, in a way, like a research arm of the navy operating in the far north. There was also a military base in Alaska, and the navy had a submarine prowling the waters of the Arctic Ocean, just like the Russians did, but on the ice, there was no military presence. It was something like the Wild West, I imagined. There were laws, kind of, but no one to enforce them. The scientists and energy company employees and occasional coast guard and navy personnel who worked up here knitted together their own rules of behavior and kept the peace as best they could, like Captain Peterson had said.

Of course, in the Wild West, everyone had carried guns. Here, nobody on my team did. This wasn't a combat mission, and QuickFind wasn't a combat system.

So I got a little nervous when we arrived at the base that this mysterious research team had set up.

The first guy that we saw had a black automatic rifle slung over his shoulder: an AK-105, which was the standard weapon of the Russian Special Forces.

As he made his way across the ice to greet us with a friendly wave, his movements had a distinct military bearing. A lump caught in my throat.

Hansel and I weren't meeting with a team of researchers working for an oil company, even if that's what Captain Peterson thought they were. We were meeting with a team of soldiers for hire, who were maybe working for an oil company or maybe working for a foreign government. Whoever they were, though, they weren't civilians.

They were mercenaries.

05:
ON THIN ICE

THE base the mercenaries had set up looked like an alien spaceship set on stilts above the snow. It was a bright red eight-sided structure, with a crown of solar panels ringing the top, wide windows set into the walls, and retractable metal stairs leading up into its belly.

There were a few transports like ours parked around it, although whatever equipment was sitting on their flatbed trailers had been covered by tarps, so we couldn't see it. There were three snowmobiles parked by the bottom of the stairs, and two large generators and fuel tanks just off to the side.

As I climbed down from the trailer bed, the captain beckoned me over to meet the men who were climbing down from the base. The man with the gun quickly stepped away and disappeared inside. I couldn't help but think he was reacting just like an enlisted man did when officers arrived. Every minute made me feel more certain these were military men, and that certainty made every minute feel longer and more dangerous. Hansel watched me from his crate and barked nervously. I glanced back and gave him the signal to lie down and wait. He fell silent and obeyed, comforted by the familiar instructions in a place that was so unfamiliar.

I envied him. I wished someone was there to give me clear instructions. My confidence was beginning to waver.

"Captain Peterson, how nice to see you again," one of the mercenaries said, stepping up and shaking the captain's hand. He wore heavy cargo pants and a white parka with the logo of his company stitched across the breast pocket and the sleeves. I didn't recognize it. His wraparound sunglasses hid his eyes, better than his polite words hid his true feelings.

"You as well, Nicolás," the captain said. "I'd like you to meet Marine Mammal Handler Ryan Keene, on loan to us from the United States Navy."

I stuck out my hand and saw a twitch of eyebrow over the frame of the man's sunglasses. He pursed his lips. "So the United States Navy has taken over your operation? Are we in a military zone now, Captain?"

"No, no, Nicolás," the captain reassured him. "Ryan and his team are here to assist us in recovering our lost equipment, that's all. I wanted you to meet first so that you didn't think we were up to anything suspicious. I wanted to avoid confusion like we had earlier. Once he and his sea lion have performed their duties, they'll be back on their way to the States."

Nicolás paused, then his suntanned face broke into a smile. "You are welcome here, sir," he said, finally grabbing my hand and pumping it enthusiastically.

I decided to let him call me *sir*. I figured it couldn't hurt to have this mercenary think me more powerful than I was. I noticed Captain Peterson didn't correct him, either. The politeness these two men showed each other concealed a deep distrust, and it didn't conceal it well. They were just playing at friendliness, and the peace was a lot thinner than the ice on which we stood.

"So you will send a sea lion to find what you have lost," he said. "And this sea lion knows what it looks like?"

"He's been trained to identify certain objects," I said vaguely. I didn't want to give this guy too much information.

"Fascinating." The man smiled again. "Some of us would be very interested to watch him work. With your permission, of course."

"We'd be glad to have you," said the captain.

My eyes bulged behind my own sunglasses, but the captain couldn't see them and I kept my face as neutral as possible. I didn't want to contradict Captain Peterson openly — he was the boss here, after all — but I was not okay with letting these men come along to watch us work. The Marine Mammal Program had only been declassified by the military in the 1990s, and there was a lot we could do that I didn't think we needed to show to foreign mercenaries, whether they were friends or foes. Hansel's skills were an advantage up here, and I didn't want to give that advantage away.

But I kept my mouth shut. It was the captain's decision, not mine.

"Wonderful," Nicolás replied. "We will follow you to the site. In fact, I should tell you I've had a few of my colleagues camping there since your last visit, to make sure the location remained secure. We wouldn't want anyone to interfere with your research."

"I appreciate that," said the captain. "But it really wasn't necessary."

The man shrugged. "How will we thrive so far north without helping each other from time to time?"

"Thank you," the captain told him. "Then we'll be on our way."

We all shook hands again, and Nicolás turned and shouted out instructions to his men. He spoke Spanish to some of them and then, I noticed, said a bunch of other things in a language I didn't know but I guessed was Russian.

As we returned to our trucks, I stopped Captain Peterson. "What else do you know about these guys?"

"Nicolás and his top people are Venezuelan," he said. "A few of the others are Russian. Their company, from what a search on the Internet told me, is based in Dubai and provides support for oil exploration."

"Support?"

The captain shrugged. "It's unclear what that means, but I'm no fool. I see they aren't simple research-ers. We're right on the line between Russian waters and American waters, and it's debatable who has a right to the ocean floor below us. I believe some of these men really are researchers for a legitimate oil company. I believe they also report back to the authorities in Moscow. It's a tense situation and nobody trusts each other."

"And you told none of this to the navy when you requested our help?" I demanded.

The captain cleared his throat. "In my request to your commanders, I explained all of this. What they chose to share with you or not to share with you was out of my control."

I spat on the ground at my feet and shook my head. I felt like a pawn in a much bigger game of chess, a pawn who hadn't even realized he was part of someone else's game. I should've known, of course. The navy used its pieces how it saw fit, and I was a tiny one. My superior officers had decided not to tell me what a dangerous situation we were wandering into.

I couldn't let that stop me from doing my job,

though. Whoever these mercenaries were and whatever they were up to wasn't my problem. My job was to recover the equipment for the R/V *Buzz Aldrin*, keep my sea lion safe, and return to California with a report of mission accomplished. Anything else was way above my pay grade.

"Do me a favor, Captain," I said.

"What is it?" he asked.

"Before we head out, let them know, no guns."

"No guns?" he said. "There are polar bears in this region. You might want a few guns around to protect Hansel. We keep a high-powered rifle in our vehicle at all times."

"No guns," I repeated. "They claim not to be soldiers, then they shouldn't come armed like soldiers."

"I will pass along your request, *sailor*," the captain said, a reminder that he had the authority here, not me. He sounded a lot like any other officer all of a sudden.

"Thank you, *sir*," I said, and turned back to Hansel in his crate.

Like he'd said, it really was a tense situation all around. I would later wish that I hadn't made it even worse when we got to the water's edge, but regrets are like melting ice. Stay too long on them and you'll fall in and drown.

06:
SALVAGE

I was another hour's drive to the large crack in the sea ice where the R/V *Buzz Aldrin*'s equipment had been lost. From a mile away, I could see the high gantry crane that hung over the exposed water. I knew that must have been part of the structure that broke, and as we got closer, I could see that it was tilted slightly in the ice, like it had begun to fall.

Beside it, there was a tent, and three guys stood outside next to two snowmobiles, awaiting our arrival. They had a trailer hitched to one of their snowmobiles, and it had a rack of scuba tanks on it, along with a few other crates of supplies. These were Nicolás's men and they looked like they'd been up here awhile.

They also must not have gotten my message, even though I saw they had a big radio antenna sticking up from their campsite. They had weapons on them, automatic rifles just like the mercenary back at their base. They didn't look like they were about to set them aside, either.

I put my fingers through the bars of Hansel's cage and scratched his neck. The feeling of his fur calmed my nerves, but I still had a very bad feeling about what we were driving into. I resolved to get my job over with as fast as I could. They didn't call us the QuickFind System for nothing. We'd be quick, and then we'd be home again.

Still, as we started unloading our gear, I whispered to Bryson, "Keep an eye on those guys. I don't want them too close."

Bryson nodded and continued to set up our small boat. Kincaid, Bryson, and I would deploy with Hansel and our pulley system on the boat, while Dr. Morris waited back on the ice with the others, standing by to assist if Hansel had a medical emergency. I saw Nicolás whispering with some of his men, nodding in our direction. He pointed at Hansel and one of his men, a big fellow with close-cropped blond hair and a nose that looked like it'd been broken more than once, shook his head about whatever his boss had said. I didn't like the way his eyes traveled over Hansel, like he was sizing up my sea lion for a meal. He reminded me of a bad guy in an action movie, the kind of bad guy who never got a name, no matter how many terrible things he did. A nameless killer.

The sooner we got away from these guys the better.

I opened Hansel's crate and let him climb onto the boat. There was a pad beside a soft bench along the starboard side, where he knew to wait. The moment he clambered onto it, he flopped down onto his belly. He looked like a giant furry slug in a blue utility vest with the face of a dog and the fins of a dolphin. It was hard not to smile when looking at such an amazingly absurd, brilliant animal.

The mercenaries, I noticed, were not smiling.

"Okay, Captain," I announced when we were ready. "We've got four pieces of equipment on this request form, and you will have four pieces of equipment returned to you right away."

"I look forward to seeing you in action," he responded, as friendly as ever, but I could see he was nervous, too. In spite of the cold, a trickle of sweat made its way from his right temple down his cheek. It's never a good thing for the enlisted men when the captain breaks a sweat.

I climbed aboard and shoved off from the edge of the ice onto the calm, cold Arctic water.

These wide channels that opened up in the sea ice every spring and summer were called leads, and they came in all different shapes and sizes, opening and closing all the time. Many an unfortunate Arctic explorer in the olden days had starved to death on his ship when a lead had closed and trapped him in the ice.

This lead was a medium-sized one, about a hundred yards across to the other side, which was like a riverbank made of ice. I glanced over at it, thinking about the polar bears the captain had mentioned. I figured they'd keep their distance from this many humans, but one never knew.

I'd read how at this time of year, as the ice begins to melt, it becomes harder and harder for the big bears to find enough food. A hungry bear might just risk coming near a bunch of humans if it meant a nice tasty meal of California sea lion. I wished I'd brought that rifle out on the boat with me. We had a flare gun, I remembered, which would probably scare a bear off if it came to that. As Kincaid drove us out to the center of the lead, I flipped open the flare gun's case, just to make myself feel better. It was in there, along with three colored smoke grenades, the kind used to tell helicopters where to land in an emergency evacuation. I bet a bear wouldn't like those, either.

Once Kincaid shut off the engines, I gave Hansel a pat on the head.

"Okay, buddy, it's time to go to work."

Hansel popped up onto his front flippers. His nose worked the air and his little ear flaps perked up. I pulled the orange whistle I carried around my neck out from under my coat, then took the lid off a bucket of chopped fish parts and tossed one to him.

He caught it in his mouth, chewed once, and swallowed it. I heard a cheer from the shore and looked back to see Captain Peterson's men applauding as they watched us. If they thought that was remarkable, they'd really be amazed by what we did next.

I admit it, I felt the need to show off.

I raised my arm up and gave two short blasts of the whistle, then I swept my arm out in a wide arc, and Hansel flung himself sideways, tail over head, into the water with a splash. He popped his head back up again, bobbing like a furry buoy beside the boat and giving a triumphant bark. I made the QuickFind signal, careful to block the view from shore so the mercenaries couldn't see the exact gesture. I didn't want them knowing all the navy's secrets.

In a flash, Hansel was off and away, diving low to hunt down the lost objects. After only a few minutes, he popped back to the surface and barked three times to tell me he'd located the third of the objects I'd asked him to find. We'd trained him to identify them in a certain order, but he didn't need to find them in that order. I praised him in a cheerful voice, then knelt down and held out a triangular bite plate, with a big metal clamp attached to the front of it. This was the main tool of the QuickFind System.

Hansel would dive back down to the object he'd found and bite down on the plate to open the clamp, which he would then attach to the object, letting up his bite to close the metal clamp again. Then he would give three tugs to the attached line to make sure it was secure, and come back to the boat to get his reward. After that, we'd drive back to the ice, hook the line to a heavy-duty winch system, and they'd haul the item to the surface.

At my signal, off Hansel went, and I checked my paperwork to see which item he'd found first. It was a large drill bit, designed to dig out samples of the seafloor that the crew of the *Buzz Aldrin* could analyze.

Moments later, he was back, no clamp in his mouth. He hopped on board, and I gave him a fish and a rub-down. We drove back to the edge of the ice, and Bryson unhooked the line that went from the undersea clamp to our boat and handed it to the crew onshore. While they hooked it up to their system to pull the drill up, we went back out to repeat the process for another object.

I noticed the mercenaries whispering to each other. Nicolás said something into his walkie-talkie.

In almost no time, Hansel found the second and fourth objects — a sample collection crate and some sort of motor. The team onshore hauled them up.

I sent him for the final object, and nearly ten minutes passed before Hansel returned. He didn't bark, though, just jumped from the water and put his head down on his pad. This was his unique way of apologizing. He made the kind of face a kid makes when begging to get out of a test and have recess instead.

The captain's voice crackled through the radio. "No luck on the last item?"

"Luck's got nothing to do with it," I told him. I could see the mercenaries starting to pack up their campsite. They figured we were done.

I checked my watch. We'd been at it for a while now, and the water was very cold. I worried Hansel was beginning to tire or to freeze.

"You okay, pal?" I asked him.

He stared at me with his big black eyes wide. He wanted only to please. He wanted only to succeed. The moment I spoke to him, he popped back up and slid into the water again.

He wasn't ready to quit. He hadn't been able to find the last object, but that didn't mean he wanted to give up.

There was a reason we were such a good team.

"We're going down one more time," I said. I signaled for Hansel to search again for that final object.

The mercenaries stopped loading their things, and Nicolás watched me with his lips frozen in a half smile. The blond man beside him moved slightly away. It looked for all the world to me like they were fanning out into a defensive position.

What, I wondered, were they afraid we'd find down there?

07:
A BAD BREAK

HANSEL reappeared seven minutes later. He'd been down a long time, but his staccato bark told me he'd found object number one, the missing piece we'd been looking for. I gave him the clamp, and he vanished below the surface. It only took him about two minutes to go back to where he'd found the item and attach it, and with a few flicks of his mighty tail fin, he was back, leaping on board and shaking icy water from his fur, splashing the rest of us in the process. The boat rocked.

"Nice job, Hansel!" I held my palm up and he raised a fin to give me five. Then I gave him a fish and Kincaid started the motor to bring us back to the ice so the team could haul in their equipment. Mission accomplished.

I wrapped Hansel in a heat blanket while they started the winch. The motor rumbled and spit black smoke as the heavy cord wrapped around the spool. As we waited, Dr. Morris came over and took Hansel's temperature, looked in his mouth, checked his heart rate.

"He's been straining a little with the effort and the cold," she said. "But he seems good to go. Impressive."

"Hansel's an elite athlete," I told her. "He could do ten of these missions."

"Don't push it," she said.

A minute later, the large object broke the surface and the crane hoisted it into the air. The mercenaries moved in around the research team to get a better look.

I suddenly noticed they'd spread out to flank us all, the navy guys *and* the researchers from the *Buzz Aldrin*. I didn't like it, but there wasn't much I could do about it.

"That what you were looking for?" I asked Captain Peterson.

"It is," he confirmed. "This is the data recorder. Soil analysis, mapping data, cameras, and microphones — all the records of our research are on here. It's the gold mine, and you got it back for us."

"Just doing our job," I told him. "Now it's probably best if we get out of here."

"Captain!" one of his researchers called out from beside the data-recording device. "Look at this."

The captain stepped over to the big boxy object. I followed with Hansel, curious.

"It looks like this piece was sawed off," the man said. He pointed to where some kind of metal arm that attached to the drill bit had been cut. There were also deep gouges and scorch marks in the metal around the door to the locked data port, like someone had been trying to break into it. The researcher dropped his voice to a whisper. "Someone did this on purpose. They wanted to get into the data port, and when that failed, they cut the whole thing loose."

"You're saying . . ." The captain dropped his voice as well. "Sabotage?"

The man nodded. I felt a nervous churning in my stomach. "Our logo is gone, too," he added. "Scratched off, maybe."

Nicolás was suddenly by our side. "Captain," he said, his teeth bared in a crocodile smile. "You were right — a very impressive sea lion. However, I think he has made a mistake. This device does not belong to you."

"Excuse me?" I said. "Hansel does not make mistakes."

Nicolás peeled off his sunglasses and his ice-blue eyes met mine. "He has found a device that belongs to my team," he told me. "As you can see."

He bent down beside the object, lifting up one side to reveal a sticker of the same logo he had on his jacket. It was obvious it had been placed there recently. Who puts a sticker on a piece of undersea research equipment? This wasn't a middle-school science fair project. Who did he think he was kidding?

"This is our equipment, unfortunately," he said. The set of his face told me that he didn't actually think he was kidding anyone and he didn't care. He probably figured he had the firepower to back just about any claim he cared to make. "It seems your sea lion has gone out of his way to succeed, but caused you to damage our research in the process."

"Impossible," I replied.

"And yet the evidence is in front of you," Nicolás answered me coolly.

"You had divers here for days before we arrived," I argued back, which I really shouldn't have done. "You could have put that *sticker* on there yourselves."

I said the word *sticker* the way a person might say *booger*.

Nicolás laughed. "And why would we have done that?"

"Maybe you were trying to steal it when it broke off and you lost it," I said. "Maybe you sabotaged it and hoped it wouldn't be found, but decided to have a backup plan in case we did find it."

"Captain." Nicolás sighed. "Your sea lion tamer has some wild conspiracy theories. Remarkable for someone who had no idea what this object did even ten minutes ago."

"I am *not* a sea lion tamer," I said. He'd used a circus term to mock me. "And I *know* my sea lion found the right object. This is what was lost and this is what we found."

"You're very agitated." Nicolás was patronizing me.

"You have serial numbers, Captain?" I asked. "Can't you check the serial number for this machine against your records? If it matches, then we'll know he's lying."

Captain Peterson held his hands up, trying to keep the peace. "Now before we start accusing each other —"

"You know, I had believed this was the honest mistake of a simple animal," Nicolás said, his eyes still locked on mine. "But now I think perhaps it is a scheme for *you* to steal *our* equipment."

The men with the guns started to close their semicircle in around us. We were outnumbered and outgunned and the situation was getting worse, but I had no intention of backing down.

"No one is trying to steal anything," the captain said. "I'm sure this misunderstanding can be worked out and we can all continue our research in peace. We'll simply secure the device until we can each verify the serial numbers."

"Who will secure the device?" Nicolás growled. "We do not believe these men from your military can be trusted. Perhaps this is the start of an invasion?"

"Invasion? Are you kidding me?" I scoffed. I probably shouldn't have scoffed. "If anyone is *invading*, it's you! You're the ones who came armed!"

"Yes," said Nicolás, his voice colder than the ice all around us. "We did."

"Come on, Captain," I said. "We should take this item of yours and get out of here."

I turned to go, and Nicolás grabbed my shoulder to stop me.

Hansel's whole body quivered. He let out an agitated bark, then used his powerful front flippers to push himself off the ice. It happened faster than any of us could react.

His jaws clamped around Nicolás's forearm and slammed shut, his big teeth ripping through the man's parka.

"Ahh!" Nicolás shouted, falling backward as Hansel's full weight knocked him down.

"Hansel!" I yelled, just as the blond mercenary spun his rifle around and leveled it at Hansel's head. "No!"

Instead of pushing Hansel off, I sprang for the nameless mercenary and tackled him from the side just as his finger squeezed the trigger.

A shot cracked the Arctic air. Both of us hit the hard ice with a thud, but the mercenary was trained in combat, while I'd only had the basic navy recruit course. Before I could even figure out that I'd landed on him, he'd brought a knee into my stomach and slammed his fist into the side of my head. My ears rang and I found myself suddenly on my back, looking up at the barrel of his gun pointed directly at my face. I glanced over and saw Hansel exactly where I'd last seen him, on top of Nicolás, biting his arm.

The Nameless One yelled at me but I didn't understand him.

"He's telling you to call off your sea lion," Nicolás said, his voice strained with the pain in his arm and Hansel's weight on his chest.

"Tell him to get that gun out of my face!" I yelled back.

Nicolás passed along my instructions in Russian, and the blond guy lowered his gun. I blew my whistle and Hansel let go, bounding off of Nicolás and coming to my side. I rolled onto my hands and knees and then pushed myself up to standing.

The rest of the mercenaries had their guns pointed at us.

"Okay, everybody, just calm down," Captain Peterson said. "This got out of hand, but we can fix this. There's a Finnish naval station a few miles from here. We'll turn the device over to them and they can mediate our dispute. There is no need for things to turn violent."

"Of course not," said Nicolás. "We all want to maintain the peace."

"Then please start by lowering your weapons," the captain said.

Nicolás nodded. "Apologies." He rolled back his sleeve and I winced, seeing that his forearm was bright red, dripping with blood. Hansel had done some damage, and it was amazing that the man wasn't howling with pain. He was tough, that was clear, and had probably been trained to deal with a lot of agony. It made me trust him even less, if that was possible.

"We can have our doctor stitch that up for you," the captain said.

"No need," said Nicolás. "We have our own medic. I ask only one thing: that you disarm yourselves as well."

The captain looked around, confused. "We're not armed."

"You have a weapon," Nicolás replied. "And I would like it put down."

He nodded toward Hansel.

"What?" I balked. "No."

Put down was the gentle way of saying *executed*. He wanted to kill Hansel.

"He is a danger and has attacked me, unprovoked," the man said. "Not only did he damage our sensitive research equipment" — Nicolás paused to see if we'd object — "but he caused me serious harm, as you see. My men and I do not feel safe with him in our area of operations. I repeat: He must be put down."

"You can't." I turned to the captain. "Hansel is a part of the United States Navy's Marine Mammal Program, a member of our team, and you have no authority to do this to him."

The captain nodded, but didn't look at me. He spoke directly to Nicolás. He looked grim. "I'll have to communicate with his superiors. The navy will need to sign off on this. It's not a decision I can make myself, you understand?"

"I understand," said Nicolás. "I hope you explain to them the seriousness of the crime that has been committed against me. I would hate to have to file a formal complaint with the United Nations about this violation."

"I will make your position clear," the captain told him.

"And what about ours?" I objected.

"I will explain the situation to them clearly and fairly," the captain snapped at me.

"Until you do," Nicolás suggested, "perhaps we all stay here, with the sea lion under guard."

The captain considered.

"Captain Peterson," I complained. "You can't do this. I cannot allow —"

"Listen here, Keene," the captain interrupted me. "This situation got out of hand and it is now bigger than us, bigger than you and your sea lion. I will call up your commander, and we will decide what is best for the mission and the interests of the United States in the Arctic region, and you will receive your orders. Understood?"

"I —"

His face reddened. He'd turned his anger at the situation onto me. "Is that understood, sailor?"

"Yes, *sir*," I told him. "I request permission to stay with Hansel while we wait."

"Granted," said the captain. He was probably relieved to have me out of his way.

I rested my hand on Hansel's head. The poor guy had no idea what was going on. He knew only that he'd felt I was in danger and he'd protected me. It had been instinct. He hadn't meant to cause problems. And yet now, in a matter of minutes, he'd gone from the hero of the mission to a criminal awaiting execution or pardon on the orders of some officers several thousand miles away.

I couldn't help but think that was what Nicolás and his men had wanted all along.

08:
AWAITING ORDERS

WE set up a tent beside Hansel's crate. Bryson and I stayed, while Kincaid and Dr. Morris returned to the *Buzz Aldrin* with the captain and his people. Nicolás, the blond mercenary, and one other guy also stayed behind, setting their tent back up on the other side of Hansel's crate. We all had our eyes on my sea lion, on the disputed data recorder, and on each other. We were all waiting for morning.

Of course, it would be hard to know when morning had come. At this time of year, north of the Arctic Circle, the sun stayed above the horizon all day. It never set, just rotated around the horizon like a glow-ing basketball spinning on the rim of the net but never falling in. There would be no darkness, only our shad-ows stretching around us hour after daylight hour. The mercenaries and I would have a full sunlit night to stare icicles at each other.

For Hansel's sake, I'd covered his crate with a heavy blanket, so that he would still experience the dark of night and could rest. I climbed under the blan-ket with him, ignoring the objections from the others, and braced myself against his natural stench.

He was snoozing happily on his belly in his crate but looked up at me without moving when I sat down in front of the opening.

"Don't worry, buddy," I told him. "The navy looks after their own. They're not going to let these goons do anything to you."

His eyes stared back at me, impassive. How could a sea lion understand that his life was in the hands of some officers back in California or maybe even at the

Pentagon in Virginia? How could he understand the complicated politics of Arctic territory? In truth, I wasn't sure I understood them myself.

I knew that the North Pole and the waters around it were considered international waters and couldn't be claimed by any nation, but that there were five countries disputing the rest of the territory under all kinds of laws and rules. Countries are allowed to claim the area twelve nautical miles off their coasts as "national waters," like they're a part of the country itself, and they're allowed to pursue economic activity up to two hundred nautical miles off their shores, which meant things like shipping and also drilling for oil. The problem was that they could also claim exclusive rights to any area of the ocean floor connected to their continental shelf.

The Arctic seafloor hadn't been mapped all that well over the years, as it had been covered in ice, but now that the ice was melting more and more, nations were racing to plant their flags on the ocean floor and gain control of the valuable oil below. In this sea, where Alaska and Russia were so terribly close, the fight was to see who could show a strong claim to the ocean floor first. The weapons may have been soil samples and satellite pictures, but it was a fight nonetheless, and it seemed that this one data box from the *Buzz Aldrin* had become dangerous. Whatever it had found, the mercenary team wanted it for themselves. Or at least, they didn't want the United States to have it. I was more convinced than ever that these guys were working for the Russian government, or at least a Russian oil company, which was basically the same thing.

Suddenly, my dark tent underneath Hansel's blanket flooded with light. Bryson slid underneath to join us. I was momentarily blinded, until he let the blanket fall again and we sat side by side in front of Hansel's crate.

"Can you believe it?" Bryson asked. "It's three in the morning and it's bright as noon out there."

"What are you doing awake?" I asked.

"It's your turn to sleep," he told me. "It's my shift to watch Hansel now."

"I'm okay."

"No," Bryson told me. "You need your rest. We're going to have a long day tomorrow packing up all this nonsense and getting ready to go home."

I nodded. He had total faith that the navy wasn't about to let some mercenaries kill my sea lion or steal sensitive research data. He figured the commanders would sort everything out with a few phone calls and by this time tomorrow we'd be asleep in our berths on board the *Buzz Aldrin*, waiting for the chopper to come back and take us to the mainland.

I agreed.

I wished Hansel a good night and trudged back outside into the nighttime sun. Inside their tent, two of the mercenaries were playing on an Xbox they'd hooked up to their generator. They didn't offer to let us play. The blond mercenary, who I now thought of as the Nameless One, was outside, sitting on a crate, wrapped in his parka, his rifle resting beside him. He had on his sunglasses and was so still I thought he might have fallen asleep sitting up, until he spoke to me.

I didn't have any idea what he said, because he said it in Russian. But he ended it with a laugh and pointed behind me over the crack in the ice. I turned to see where he was pointing: On the other side of the lead in the ice, a big polar bear stalked the water's edge with two cubs behind it. The mama bear looked across at us, lifted one paw and sniffed the air, then continued on. One of her cubs stopped to imitate her, his own fuzzy paw up, but was knocked over by the cub behind him, who hadn't stopped and smacked right into him. They both rolled around playfully with each other, until the mama bear turned and made a chuffing sound loud enough for us to hear on our side of the ice. The bear cubs stopped playing and resumed their single-file march along the ice.

The Nameless One said something else to me, and I saw the second polar bear, bigger than the mama bear, but far away, following them from a distance. I wondered if that was papa bear, except the way he had his eyes fixed on those cubs as he moved made me think he wasn't following them so much as *stalking* them. He was hunting his own kind.

"Yum-yum for bear," Nameless said to me, and pointed to Hansel's blanket-draped crate.

He thought I'd just let them shoot Hansel and leave his corpse for the bears.

He had another think coming. I wasn't about to let Hansel go without a fight, and neither was the United States Navy. We did not abandon our own.

Unfortunately, the next morning, I'd find that only half of what I'd thought was true.

The captain returned with the news that the navy had decided, after a formal request from Nicolás's government, in the interest of peaceful cooperation in the Arctic Circle, to allow Hansel to be put down. He was considered equipment, after all, not a person with rights.

If anyone was going to fight for Hansel, I realized, it would have to be me, alone.

09:
EXECUTE ORDER

"**CAPTAIN,**" I told him, my heart leaping into my throat. "They can't do this."

"I have the orders right here," Captain Peterson told me, showing me the printout from the office of the rear admiral in charge of the Space and Naval Warfare Systems Command. He was my boss's boss's boss. And he had authorized Hansel's execution.

"Dog catchers do it all the time," he tried to explain to me. "When a dog bites a neighbor, the dog gets put down. It's not the dog's fault, but it keeps the neighborhood from falling apart. That's what we're trying to do here. The US is in the middle of some tough negotiations up here, and if this incident becomes a full-blown violent conflict, there is no telling where it will stop."

"But it's all a lie," I said. "They're trying to steal that data, and they're using Hansel to distract us from that."

"Son, you have your orders," the captain told me.

"I cannot obey them," I replied. Suddenly, Dr. Morris, Bryson, and Kincaid were at my side.

"He's right. Under the Marine Mammal Protection Act, we cannot endanger the animals under our care," Dr. Morris explained. "There is no authority that can order Hansel to be put down for any reason other than medical necessity."

"That's true!" I said. I'd forgotten that it wasn't just morally wrong to kill Hansel, it was *legally* wrong. If we let them kill Hansel while he was under our care, we'd be breaking the law.

"That is a United States law," Nicolás cut in to our

conversation. He'd been listening to us the whole time. I also noticed his men had surrounded us again. He'd brought back three more guys than he'd had before. All of them were armed. We never should have let them flank us like that, but there wasn't a combat soldier among us. We were trained to look after a sea lion, not prevent an ambush.

"We are in international territory now," Nicolás explained. "United States law does not apply. I will allow you to perform the act yourself if you wish, but it must be done and it must be done now. We will not wait here any longer." He made a show of checking his watch.

The captain looked around the semicircle of armed men. I could tell he was conflicted. I could tell he didn't want to go through with this. I could also tell he wasn't brave enough to stop it, either. He was a peacemaker who didn't realize we were already fighting an invisible war.

He called for one of his men to bring over their high-powered rifle, and he put it in my hands. "It's the only way, sailor."

My hands shook as I took the rifle from him. I could see the Nameless One smirking as I crossed slowly to Hansel's cage. Time seemed to slow down, like in a movie. Bryson opened the cage for me, and Hansel bounced out as excited as ever. He had his vest on, like he was going to go for another swim, another search, another prize.

But there would be no more prizes.

I didn't even stop to wonder why someone had put his vest on him while I was asleep.

"Let me make sure he's relaxed," Dr. Morris said loudly so that everyone could hear. It seemed like a strange thing to say. Hansel looked pretty relaxed already. He had no idea what was coming.

Dr. Morris bent down next to him and ran her hands over Hansel's head and chest, examined his flippers, and pulled his lips up to examine his big teeth, which were impressive. Everyone looked at them.

And that must have been Dr. Morris's plan, because I saw her other hand slip a small plastic Baggie into the waterproof pocket on the back of Hansel's vest, and inside that Baggie was a thumb drive, the kind that you could use to copy data and transfer it between computers. Dr. Morris's eyes met mine and she gave the slightest of winks.

She'd downloaded the data from the device while everyone was paying attention to me. That's why she'd joined our argument late.

"All *Finnish*," she said, staring right at me.

Not *finished*.

Finnish.

She was telling me to get that data to the Finnish research station. She was telling me to get Hansel there, too.

But how was I supposed to do that, surrounded by armed men, with no support from the navy, and with miles and miles of Arctic ice between here and there?

I saw Kincaid's head cock to the side. Our boat was still in the water, tied up on the ice behind me; the keys were in the ignition. One of the emergency-supply backpacks was sitting next to the motor, tucked low in the hull so it wasn't obvious.

She and the veterinarian must have been planning this all night, the moment they heard the navy's decision. They wanted me to make a break for it. But how?

"Well, son," the captain said. "Let's not drag this out."

"You can't do this," Bryson whispered to me, his eyes pleading. He had no idea what Dr. Morris and Kincaid had planned, and he hadn't figured out their clues. It was probably better that way. I was about to violate a direct order from an admiral. I didn't need to ruin Bryson's career, too.

"He has to do it." Dr. Morris put her hand on Bryson's shoulder and pulled him gently away from me. She met my eyes. "We don't want to fuel any more trouble here. Be quick about it."

Fuel? Be quick? She gave me a slow nod.

And then I saw what she meant.

I raised the rifle. The mercenaries backed up a little, clearing out of the line of fire in case I missed. I stared through the scope, and Hansel's big brown snout filled my vision. I lifted the barrel slightly, leveling it at his eye. My hands shook as I rested my finger on the trigger. Hansel, ever obedient, stayed put, no doubt uncertain about why I was pointing this thing at him, but not at all frightened by it. He trusted me completely, trusted that I would never put him in harm's way.

And he was right.

I lifted the rifle higher and set my sight on the fuel tank by the mercenaries' generator.

I took a deep breath and let out half of it.

My hands steadied.

No going back now.

I squeezed the trigger and the crack of the rifle echoed across the ice.

There was a terrible still moment when Hansel cocked his head at me and the mercenaries wrinkled their brows.

"What are you —?" Nicolás began, but he never got to finish his sentence.

The gas explosion that followed sent everyone diving for cover. A pillar of flame and smoke shot high into the pale white sky.

"Hansel!" I yelled, and blew a quick blast on my whistle.

My sea lion followed me at a full run on his flippers, his body heaving and bouncing awkwardly as we leapt together into the boat and cut free from shore before the mercenaries could get back on their feet.

I ordered Hansel to lie down low in the hull as I throttled the engine and sped from the burning debris on the ice.

I hadn't made it far when the mercenaries opened fire.

10:
UNDER FIRE, UNDER WATER

I'D never been shot at before. I could hear the whistle of the bullets and the crack of the shots as if they were right next to me, but somehow, it wasn't scary. I was so focused on getting Hansel to safety that I didn't worry for myself. I knew how to drive the boat, and that knowledge was what I focused on. I didn't think about dying. I thought about living.

Keep moving. Move fast. Don't follow a straight line that they can target.

Water kicked up in little explosive geysers as bullets hit the surface all around the boat. I glanced over my shoulder and saw that I hadn't made it very far and that the blond guy had a pretty clear shot at me. My team was being held at gunpoint, while the Nameless One fired in my direction.

I saw the flash from the muzzle of his rifle and I ducked my head down instinctively. Bullets sliced into the hull of my boat, perforating the sides like Swiss cheese and getting dangerously close to Hansel. Another burst of gunfire punched a cluster of holes in the engine, which spluttered, spat black smoke, and died.

The Nameless One lowered his rifle and gave me a salute. He didn't need to shoot me in order to kill me. He just had to sink me into the Arctic Ocean.

The hull was filling with frigid water. Hansel would be okay in it, but I wouldn't last long before hypothermia set in. If I froze to death or drowned, the mercenaries could argue that they weren't responsible; that it had been my own fault for violating orders and running away with Hansel. I wondered if there would be a cover-up, if my death would be called an accident and everyone would keep going about their business, searching for oil, as if none of this ever happened.

They'd been willing to let Hansel die to keep the peace, why not me, too?

I saw Captain Peterson yelling at Nicolás, and Nicolás yelling back. The captain had a gun pointed in his face.

It struck me that the mercenaries could probably get rid of the rest of my team, too. They could simply eliminate all the witnesses and call it an accident. Who was up here to question them? It'd be their word against no one else's if all of us were dead.

If I sank out here, I realized, that is exactly what the mercenaries would do.

But if I escaped with the thumb drive and made it to the Finnish research station, I could prove that they'd been trying to steal the recovered data. I could testify that they had taken hostages and opened fire on me. They were little more than pirates, and piracy was a crime, even in international waters. I could get them all locked up.

I had to get away. I wasn't just Hansel's only chance for survival. I was the best hope for Dr. Morris and Bryson and Kincaid and Captain Peterson, too.

The problem was, I was sinking into Arctic waters and I was not wearing cold-water survival gear. The water had already come up to my boots, and the rate we were sinking was increasing.

"Swim back to us!" Nicolás shouted from the edge of the ice. "Swim back and you will be safe!"

Hansel looked at me, his belly sitting in the frigid water. I looked to the other side of the lead, about half a football field away. It was hard to swim in water this cold, and it'd be harder still with the survival pack, but I only had one choice.

I left the rifle in the sinking boat, grabbed the backpack, and signaled for Hansel to jump in.

He didn't hesitate before diving overboard. His

fuzzy brown head popped up beside the sinking boat and he barked. I gave him a command with a gesture that we'd practiced countless times, then I turned toward shore and gave Nicolás a gesture — one I was sure he'd understand — and then I jumped into the water, too.

It felt like a thousand knives stabbing every inch of my skin. I felt like my blood was somehow turning to ice and being set on fire at the same time. I couldn't help but let out a gasp as the cold sucked the air right out of my lungs. I feared my heart might stop beating right then, and for a moment I forgot how to swim.

My brain went into a nearly instant shutdown mode. My clothes were designed not to get waterlogged and drag me down, but they still seemed too heavy, like they were choking me. I started to thrash, to tear at them, but I couldn't get them off.

The pack floated next to me and I grabbed it. I wanted to use it to hold myself up, but it wasn't buoyant enough. Every time I tried to pull myself up with the pack, it sank and I spluttered for breath. My sunglasses fell off my face and hung on their strap around my neck. I imagined they were choking me and I tugged at them but couldn't get them off of me.

I was panicking.

Luckily, Hansel was in his element, and we'd swum together hundreds of times. He knew just what to do: just what I had told him to do. He swam up beneath me and used his body to push me toward the far shore. All I had to do was hang on to the pack with one hand and Hansel with the other, and he did all the swimming.

The feeling of his body against me brought me back to my senses. I had Hansel with me, and the sea lion and I were going to keep each other alive, no matter what.

I calmed down.

I breathed.

My ears stopped ringing, and I kicked with my legs, not to help Hansel — he was strong enough to swim for both of us — but to keep myself steady in the water, to keep my head up.

I looked back to the far shore and saw that the mercenaries weren't chasing me yet, just shouting. The exploding generator had blown up their snowmobiles, and they didn't have a boat with them. It would take them some time to get vehicles and, once they had them, more time to get around the huge lead in the ice to the other side.

So I had the advantage of time.

As long as I didn't freeze to death in the next fifteen minutes.

11:
OUT IN THE COLD

ANYONE who's ever gone outside without a jacket in winter knows what it feels like to be cold. Your fingers and toes sting a little and then go numb. Sometimes you bounce a bit to stay warm and your teeth chatter. Maybe your cheeks and your nose turn bright red and the air stings your nostrils and you can see your breath coming out like steam from a factory smokestack. Once you come inside again, a cup of hot chocolate warms you right up.

But freezing in the Arctic is something else altogether. Hypothermia comes quickly. In hypothermia, your body temperature drops from its normal 98.6 degrees Fahrenheit to lower and lower temperatures. Mild hypothermia hits when the body temperature gets below 95 degrees. That's when shivering starts and confusion sets in. But when the body temperature drops below 82 degrees, the shivering stops. Your fingers and toes go totally numb. Your blood stops flowing normally and your heart strains to beat. No cup of hot cocoa will fix you up once severe hypothermia sets in.

When the luxury ship *Titanic* sank in 1912, the water was about 28 degrees and many people died in less than fifteen minutes.

The water I was in now was around 25 degrees.

The loose layers of waterproof gear I had on protected me a little, slowing down the rate at which my body was losing heat, but they couldn't stop it altogether. Hansel pushed me along, which meant I didn't have to use a lot of energy to swim. All my energy was being used to keep me alive. I knew I wouldn't have long to raise my body temperature again the moment we got out. I tried to control my breathing, to keep calm.

I had no idea how long Hansel had been pushing me along. I felt like I'd been in the icy water for hours but also as if I'd just jumped in. Suddenly, Hansel pressed me against the edge of the ice. My instincts told me to grab the edge, and Hansel helped shove me up out of the water. My muscles cramped as I heaved myself onto the ice with all the strength in my arms and rolled onto my back, staring up at the pale sky the same color as the ice.

I could still hear the mercenaries shouting after me, although their voices were faint and, when I lifted my head, they were tiny specks in the distance, like little dots suspended in a giant ice cube. Hansel had pushed me a long way in the water, not just straight across.

Hansel leapt from the water and shook his fur out beside me. He barked. I knew if I didn't get up, I would die right there, and then so would he, but I felt so terribly tired. My brain told me it was time to sleep; my body wasn't telling me anything at all, it was so frozen. But I still had the emergency pack beside me. I'd had a short Survival, Evasion, Resistance, and Escape course after navy basic training, and it was time to use what I'd learned, use it now, or die.

Don't die, I told myself. *Just don't die.*

It was pretty sad as pep talks went, but it got me up off my back and got me moving.

My hands felt like flippers as I struggled to grip the zipper and pull the backpack open. The struggle took me precious minutes. My vision had narrowed to a tunnel of light. I felt like I was going to pass out, maybe throw up. But I couldn't stop.

Kincaid and Dr. Morris had done a great job packing the survival kit. There were dry clothes, a compact silver heat blanket, a small solar-powered stove, a map, and some other objects that I recognized but couldn't find the words for, my mind was so confused.

Dynamite. I repeated the word to myself. *Dynamite.* It had lost all meaning. What was dynamite? What was it for?

I let the strange tube fall back into the bag with a clank.

All the blood in my body was pulling away from my limbs, trying to stay near my vital organs, to keep them warm. My blood pressure was dropping so much that my heart couldn't keep the blood moving. This was how a person froze to death. I could have a stroke or a heart attack at any moment. I was afraid. I still had the presence of mind to be afraid.

The navy had trained me for this. I had to raise my body temperature.

I pulled off the soaking wet clothes. I knew the Arctic air was freezing my skin, although I couldn't feel it. Hansel gave me a funny look, probably confused why he — an animal — had on a vest, while I — a person — had stripped down naked.

The next seconds were crucial. I put on the dry clothes, wrapped myself in the heat blanket, pulled on a dry fleece hat, and tucked my knees up to my chest. This was the Heat Escape Lessening Position the navy taught us, HELP for short. I called Hansel over to me. He scuttled across the ice and sidled up next to me. The warmth of his body pressed against the emergency blanket. His fishy saltwater smell made me gag, but focused me, too. He smelled like life. As long as I could smell him, I was alive.

My thoughts started to clear. I had the backpack at my feet. One of the objects that I'd seen in the bag was a mini oxygen tank with a breathing mask on it.

I shoved my numb fingers into the bag and wrapped them around the tube-shaped tank and pulled it out, pressing the mask over my mouth and nose and turning the big knob to start the flow of air. The oxygen filled my lungs, and my vision widened almost instantly. I felt more energy coming back. I felt awake again.

I rummaged in the bag once more and found a small chemical warming pack. By cracking a little disk in the corner of it, I got the chemicals in the packet to begin to warm. I hugged it to my chest and the warmth spread through my body. My fingers began to sting and I started to shiver. These were good signs. Feeling was coming back to me. I was cold and uncomfortable, but I was alive. Discomfort meant life. The worse Hansel stank, the better I felt.

I don't know how long I sat there warming. After a time, Hansel lay down next to me to rest. Hazy clouds still covered the sun and the light neither dimmed nor brightened. I took out a pair of binoculars and looked to the campsite on the other side of the ice. The captain and my team were still there, seated on the ground now, but there were only two mercenaries guarding them. Nicolás and the Nameless One were gone, along with two others and one of our vehicles. They must have taken it to come after me.

I felt a little weak on my feet, but I couldn't rest anymore. I had to get moving now. I'd survived the water and slipped from the jaws of death-by-freezing, but my mission was far from complete. I still had to evade capture and reach the Finnish research station.

I pulled out the map. Kincaid had marked the site of the research station, but otherwise, the map didn't mean a lot to me. It was a satellite photo, but with the ice melt in the changing of the seasons, there was no way to know what the landscape would look like or what kind of cracks and leads and mountainous pressure ridges I might find along the way.

Although a perfect map wouldn't have been much help to me, either. Officers were usually the ones who did a lot of map training. I barely had any idea how to read a map. Whenever I'd needed to navigate, I just used the GPS on my phone.

I imagined one of those voice-activation commercials, pictured myself talking to my phone. *Phone,* I'd say, *please get us out of the Arctic alive.*

The thought made me laugh. I knew my phone was sitting with my stuff back on the *Buzz Aldrin*. I thought about my family, waiting for a weekly phone call from me, checking in. My mission wasn't top secret. They were used to being able to get in touch. I wondered when they would start to worry, or when my commanders back at Naval Base Point Loma in San Diego would start to worry. My people up here were all prisoners, so no call for help had gone out from them. When would a navy search party be sent for me? Hours? Days? And what would happen to Hansel if they found us?

The navy had decided to allow his execution, after all.

I looked back at the map. There were thirty miles of ice between me and the research station. I figured I could hike about fifteen miles per day on my own, but I had no idea how fast Hansel could walk across the ice. Sea lions can rotate their front flippers to walk on them on land. They can actually run, too, though they look awkward doing it, bouncing from side to side, their necks bobbing crazily.

But they can't go far. It takes a lot of energy for them to move on land. Hansel would probably need to rest a lot. It'd be faster if he could swim. If I stayed near the water's edge, we could cover more distance in a day, but still probably not the fifteen I could do if I were alone. Of course, if I were alone, I wouldn't have been in this mess to begin with.

Regardless, Hansel would have to swim. Near the water's edge I was at greater risk of running into a polar bear, and in the water he was at greater risk of running into a killer whale, but we had no choice. It looked like I only had enough emergency rations for about four days of hiking, and there was no food for Hansel in the pack. That was another reason to stay near the water.

He would have to hunt.

I hadn't a clue if he even knew how to hunt in the wild. He'd always been fed by humans.

It looked like we'd both be learning to do new things. At least we'd be learning together.

I checked my compass and set a heading that looked like it would keep us near the water's edge for a day or two, before we had to cross a wide stretch of ice. Hansel blinked his long eyelashes up at me. I bent down to rub his head and I pulled the thumb drive out of the pouch of his vest. The plastic bag had kept it dry, and I held it up between my gloved thumb and forefinger. So much trouble over such a small thing. I wondered what information it could possibly contain that the mercenaries would be willing to kill for it.

The only way to find out was to get to the Finnish research station.

"Come on, pal," I told Hansel, returning the Baggie to his vest pocket. "One foot in front of the other and we'll get there." I took a step and he watched me move. "One flipper at a time, I mean."

With a whistle, I let him jump into the water and he swam on ahead. I kept my eye on him as I walked beside the water, and I kept my ears alert, listening for the sound of approaching engines or the sudden crack of gunfire.

All I heard was the endless wind howling across the Arctic ice.

It was going to be a long hike.

12:
ALIEN LANDSCAPE

THE beginning of spring was actually a beautiful time to be hiking across the Arctic ice. What looked like a huge flat expanse of white from a distance was in truth a wild landscape of ridges and hills, canyons, and caves . . . all made from shifting sea ice. And it wasn't simply white. Up close, the colors dazzled in crystal blues and translucent grays, light greens and patches the color of fog. There were more shades of white than I ever imagined existed.

At one point, I had to stray from the water's edge to make my way around a massive formation of jagged ice pillars. I scrambled over a boulder that looked like a big diamond and I stood on top of it, taking in the view all around me. The ocean was below to my left and the water was so crystal clear, I could look down and see Hansel swimming, back and forth just below the surface, rolling in bored corkscrews while he waited for me to catch up. He didn't know where he was going, just that he was supposed to stay near me. I started to wonder when he'd next need to eat, and how I would tell him to hunt. But I couldn't worry about that yet.

I looked back in the direction from which I'd come and saw my own footprints, the only ones there on this strange frozen land. I felt like an astronaut on the moon . . . like Buzz Aldrin, actually. I guess that's why they'd named their research ship after him. He was the second person to walk on the moon. I wondered if I was the first to walk on this part of the frozen sea.

In the far distance behind me, still on the other side of the water from where I was, I saw a snowmobile speeding in my direction. Though the figure driving it was no bigger than an ant, I could tell by the way he leaned forward and by the rifle poking up from behind his back that it was the Nameless One. I took a look through my binoculars and confirmed it. He was living up to my idea of him as the bad guy in an action movie . . . which meant I was the hero.

I liked that thought.

He hadn't found a way to cross the water to reach me yet, and the jagged landscape was slowing his snowmobile down. Some ways behind him, clunking along on its treads, crunching over the rough ground, was the big transport vehicle. I saw the glint of sun off its windshield, and I lowered my binoculars again. I didn't need to be able to see inside to know it was Nicolás and more of his men in there. They were all coming after me, and from where I stood up on the boulder, they could see me as clearly as I could see them.

On my side of the ice, luckily a few miles away, I saw the mama polar bear and her cubs, and the big male bear following them at a distance. I hoped he'd keep his distance from me, too. I wasn't interested in getting any closer to wild polar bears than I was already.

I checked my map again and climbed down from the boulder. There was a ravine a few yards ahead that ran parallel to the water. It seemed to have been created by two ice floes bashing into each other and pulling apart over and over for several winters. The layers of the ice were different colors from the different ages when they'd frozen and refrozen. There was even a thin layer stained green and red from frozen blooms of algae.

Nicolás wouldn't be able to see me in this ravine, but neither would Hansel. My sea lion had good enough hearing and vision, though, that I'd be able to call him back to me once I got out of the ravine again. It was my best chance for throwing the mercenaries off my trail.

I shimmied down between the high walls of ice. They rose at least three feet over my head and curled around like two waves about to crash into each other. The white sky became a narrow slit overhead. I took a deep breath and let the cold air sting my nose and sharpen my mind. The air smelled sweet and clean. It made me think of snowball fights and downhill sled races. I can't explain why, but it comforted me. Enclosed in a frozen tunnel that stretched on ahead of me for who knows how long, I felt safe for the first time in hours.

The feeling didn't last.

I realized I was down in this ravine with no way out again but forward and, if that big bear came along, I wouldn't have anywhere to run. He'd be able to jump down and eat me before I could so much as scream. I began to doubt my choice to jump down here. What had I been thinking? This environment wasn't forgiving of mistakes, and I might have just made a fatal one.

I tried to catch the upper lip of the ravine and pull myself out again, but my hand slipped off and I fell back down, sliding like a skateboarder falling on a half-pipe. I picked myself up and tried again.

Some ice broke off in my hand and down I went once more.

I had no choice but to stick to my first plan and keep going.

I walked carefully, stepping over piles of broken ice, testing my footing before I put all my weight down on any one spot. Some areas were slick, so I had to do a kind of penguin shuffle walk, leaning forward with legs straight as I waddled forward. I looked ridiculous, but there wasn't another living soul around to see me . . . or so I thought.

After about an hour shuffling along, taking winding turns and belly-crawling my way up steep ice inclines, squeezing through narrow cracks where the two sides of the ravine were so close they were nearly touching, I heard a noise above.

I froze.

I froze, as in I stopped moving, and I also froze as in I actually froze, because it was colder down in that ravine and only moving had kept me from noticing the chill. I started to shiver and clenched my jaw shut, terrified that even the chatter of my teeth would give me away. If it was a person up there, I didn't want them to know I was down here. If it was that polar bear, of course, he could smell me already, so it wouldn't matter much if I shivered or not.

I pressed myself against the high wall, setting my backpack down beside me and pushing my body as flat as I could against the ice, so that I was underneath the overhang above. Maybe whatever was up there would look down and not be able to see me. Maybe it would go away.

It didn't.

13:

DINNER FOR TWO

I HEARD movement, and a flurry of snow fell as a large creature moved above my hiding place, grunting. I could hear it sniff the air. I saw the lip of ice right over my head crumbling with the weight on top of it. The animal's breath made a cloud across my tiny view of the sky. I held my own breath tight.

And then the creature barked.

"Hansel!" I cried out, stepping back into the center of the ravine and looking up at my sea lion standing proudly over me. He pointed his snout straight at me, his big eyes bright beneath his long eyelashes. He barked again, his happy bark, as if he'd just won a game of hide-and-seek we'd been playing. "You found me, buddy," I told him, laughing. "You found me."

He bounced on his front flippers and then turned away so I lost sight of him. Was he about to go off to play again? I wanted to call him. I felt better when I could see him, when he was with me, but before I could form his name on my lips, he was back. He didn't bark, though, because his mouth was full. He had two silver fish gripped in his snout and lowered his head, using the swinging motion of his long neck to toss them in a high arc straight down to me.

I had to laugh.

Not only did I not need to teach him how to hunt for fish, he'd caught some for me, too.

Before I could stop him, he sidled up to the edge of the ravine and slid himself down into it on his belly, surfing into the trough of a frozen wave until he was right next to me, wet and stinking of salt water and fish guts.

So much for the crisp clear air of the Arctic.

"I guess this is as good a place as any to make camp," I told him.

I was exhausted and hungry and I figured he was, too, because he immediately gobbled one of the fish whole — not his first of the day, I guessed by his breath. Then he laid himself out flat on the ice to rest.

I loved the idea of curling up beside him to sleep. I was so tired, although I had no clue if it was time to sleep or not. The sun was still up, of course.

I could see why early Arctic explorers went mad in this region. The endless daylight was disorienting, unrelenting, and confounding. For a person from the South — by which I mean anywhere below the Arctic Circle — life had organized itself into days divided between light and dark. We got up in the morning and worked or played or went to school in the sun. We came home, took shelter, slept when the sun went down.

But in a place where the sun didn't go down for months at a time, how did a person organize his time?

How did he decide when was night and when was day? I felt, in my confusion, the vast indifference of this polar region to my humanity. The frozen North couldn't have cared less about the needs of a person. It existed on its own terms, and it had no use for my quaint human ideas of time.

My watch told me one time, my body told me another, and the sky told me nothing at all.

I decided to listen to my body.

I would get some sleep.

But first I had to set up my camp properly.

If I didn't make a warm shelter, I'd freeze to death when my body temperature dropped in my sleep, and if I didn't eat, I'd starve to death, burning more calories trying to stay warm than I was taking in by eating. As much as I didn't feel like scaling, gutting, and cooking the fish Hansel had brought me, I knew I had to. There were some protein bars and military-issued MREs — Meals Ready to Eat — in the backpack Kincaid had prepared, but I needed to save those.

Also, I'd hate to offend Hansel, who'd gone to all the trouble of hunting for me.

I knew after I ate, I'd have to get rid of the bones and guts from the fish somehow. A polar bear could pick up the scent of blood on the breeze from miles away, and I didn't want to lure one of them here while my eyes were closed.

Being eaten alive would be a nasty way to wake up.

So I set up my tent below the overhang — in case any helicopters flew above looking for us — and I took out the solar camping stove to cook my dinner. At least the endless sunlight had one good use. The stove wouldn't have been much use in the moonlight.

I pulled out my pocketknife and drove it into the belly of the fish, slitting it from gills to guts. It was quick work ripping off the skin and pulling out the spine. Though my fingers quickly went numb, I had a nice fresh fish fillet to cook on my stove. All I was missing was a tasty butter sauce and maybe a side of roasted potatoes.

I was a few thousand miles from the nearest potato, though.

Hansel was more than happy to eat all the disgusting bits of the fish I didn't. He bestirred himself from his belly-flop spot on the ice to devour the scales and bones, then went back to sleep in front of the entrance to my tent. I had to climb over him to get in, and then I curled up under the emergency heat blanket with all my clothes still on. I set my watch to wake me in four hours, and then I slept.

In my dreams, I dreamed about a warm bed and roasted potatoes on a long dining table. At the far end of the table was Nicolás, with a covered silver tray. He whistled to get my attention and then lifted the cover to show me a thick steak laid out on the platter.

"Looks delicious," he told me. "Its name was Hansel. Have a bite."

I woke up in an ice-cold sweat half an hour before my alarm would beep. I could hear Hansel snoring outside the tent. I knew I wouldn't be going back to sleep.

It was time to pack up and get moving, because Nicolás was still coming for us and, if he caught up, I'd find my nightmare brought to life.

14:
SHADOWS

I ATE a protein bar for breakfast and set two handfuls of snow and ice onto my solar stove to melt and boil so I could drink. I had to stay hydrated if I was going to hike all day. There were a lot of bacteria and other strange things in the snow up here that I was sure wouldn't be healthy for me to drink, which is why I had to boil the water. If I got stomach cramps that kept me from walking, that would be it for me. I'd never make it. I couldn't afford to be careless, even though I felt like I was losing precious time waiting for my water to boil. There were, however, no shortcuts for Arctic survival.

Once I'd had a drink and filled my canteen, I was able to fold up the little stove, roll up the tent, and hoist the backpack up for another day of hiking.

Hansel stayed with me this time, walking on his flippers and staying right at my heels like a giant awkward puppy. I worried he'd tire quickly having to go so far on land, but he stayed with me through the ravine, even navigating over some rough patches with surprising grace. The way he moved through the inhospitable landscape without complaint or resistance reminded me that though we'd both spent our entire lives around people, he was far more a part of the natural world than I was. He had instinct to rely on, while I had pretty minimal training. As we hiked, I began to trust his instinct more than my own, and I let him go in front. Sure enough, in less than a mile, he'd found a part of the ravine that sloped back up to the top of the ice, and brought us in sight of the water again.

To get up the slope, he had to use the muscles of his neck, thrusting his whole body forward in big jolts, his back flippers stabilizing him while his front pulled him and guided him. I'm sure I looked just as clumsy, making my way up the slope on all fours to keep from sliding back down on my face.

Once we were back on the surface, I had to reorient myself to my surroundings. Although the water beside the ice looked like a river, it wasn't a river, just an opening to the ocean on which this entire ice sheet sat. It didn't flow like a river, so I couldn't use it to navigate. If I followed it, it could take me in a circle, or back to another lead and another set of ice floes, and suddenly I'd find myself a hundred miles in the wrong direction or even back where I started. I had to study the map and try to get my bearings from my compass. As smart as he was, Hansel couldn't lead us where we needed to go. I had to find our way.

While I walked along the surface, he dove back into the water, popping out occasionally to bark or grunt at me, asking for fish. When I showed him my empty hands, he'd jump back in to find his own snack if he could. Every few miles, we'd stop to rest together, but I waited until he was back in the water to eat my protein bar. I knew I'd be tempted to share with him if he saw me eating, and I couldn't afford to give up the food. Unlike Hansel, I couldn't jump in the water to hunt when I needed more to eat.

The miles stretched on and the sun still hung just above the horizon. It was an eerie feeling to walk for so long and never see my shadow shrink. These were months of permanent shadow in the Arctic and, somehow, that thought frightened me. I imagined my shadow, exhausted, simply giving up and standing still, rooting me in place where we were joined at the feet. I imagined myself stuck in it, the black shadow thick as crude oil, and me sinking into it, vanishing.

My steps grew sluggish. My legs ached from walking, but it was my mind that was exhausted. I was having crazy thoughts.

My shadow was fine. My shadow couldn't hurt me. I had to keep telling myself that.

Every few minutes, I stopped to look around me and to listen for the sound of approaching engines. The engines carried men who actually *could* hurt me. Who *wanted* to hurt me. If fear of my shadow would freeze me in place, fear of those men would keep me moving.

But I couldn't go much farther without a rest.

I sat on the ice and noticed that the air near the surface was warmer than the air up by my head when I was standing. That was because of the sun's reflection off the ice. What a strange place, I thought, where the weather could be different two feet off the ground than it was at six feet.

While I rested and considered the strangeness of the Arctic, I heard the high whine of a snowmobile engine speeding in my direction. I ducked, lying down flat to try to hide myself behind a mound of ice that was far too small to conceal me.

Hansel just stared at me, unmoving.

I motioned for him to lie down flat, too, which he did. I hoped his blue vest would provide the kind of camouflage it was meant to. As we lay there facing each other minute after minute, I realized there was no engine sound. There never had been. My mind was playing tricks on me. The isolation and the stress were getting to me. I had thought that I didn't like being around people, but being totally alone up here in the far north was driving me mad.

I stood and signaled Hansel to keep going, and we hiked on together. The poor guy must have thought I was losing it, because he stayed closer to me for a while, before he finally had had enough walking on his flippers and got back into the water.

About forty-five minutes later, on another rest, I saw the large male polar bear in the distance. He'd stopped to sniff at the sky, and our eyes met briefly. I looked around for the mama and her cubs but didn't see them. A terrible thought struck me: The bear had given up hunting them and had decided to hunt us.

I decided to cut short our rest.

As I hiked, I'd glance back every few minutes, and sure enough, the bear still followed, about three hundred yards away. Half an hour later, he was only about two hundred yards away. I'd been a kicker on the football team in high school. I was pretty good at judging distances. I pulled the flare gun out of the backpack and carried it in my hand, and put one of the smoke grenades in the pocket of my parka. If the bear got closer to me than I could kick a football on a clear day, I'd use one of them to scare him off. That'd be my last resort, though, because it'd advertise where I was to the mercenaries who were searching for me.

A while later, Hansel came back to me. The moment he reached me, he flopped down onto the ice. I checked my watch. We'd been going for about five hours, with only short rests. Hansel needed a longer rest if he was going to be able to make it for two more days of hiking. I looked back and didn't see the polar bear and hoped he'd given up, or found something else to eat. Part of me fantasized he'd dined on a small group of mercenaries and solved all my problems for me.

I sat down beside Hansel and set the flare gun across my lap, then took a big gulp from my canteen. The water was nearly frozen solid inside and what I drank was so cold it hurt my teeth. I'd have to remelt it on the solar stove later. For the moment, I just wanted to sit.

I looked up at the hazy sky and saw, up ahead, some kind of birds circling, a big flock of them. They were medium-sized white birds, with black coloring on their heads that made them look like they were wearing hats.

These were the first birds I'd seen on the ice sheet, and I sat and watched them whirl and dive. What were they diving for? I wondered.

Their high pitched *kip* and *kee-ir* shrieks weren't exactly pleasant sounds, but they were the first sounds other than Hansel's barks and snores and my own voice that'd I heard all day. I listened to them happily for a moment, before I realized they were squeaking over the sounds of loud grunts and roars coming from just on the other side of a high outcropping of ice, which formed a kind of protected cove.

I stood up from Hansel's side and walked over to an icy projection that would give me a view around the corner into the cove up ahead.

What I saw took my breath away: A herd of giant walruses filled the entire horseshoe-shaped cove in the ice. Their long tusks flashed white against their brown fur and they were bigger than any animals I'd ever seen. There were hundreds of them, sleeping and swimming, and hunting, and fighting.

To go around the walrus cove would add a full day to our journey, a day for which we didn't have enough food or energy or time. A day that would take us far from the water's edge and force Hansel to walk on land for a distance that sea lions were not meant to walk. He'd already done more walking on land than any sea lion should have to do. We couldn't go around the herd.

But I had no idea how we would get through it.

15:
LET SLEEPING WALRUSES LIE

WE rested awhile, and I gave in and pulled out a protein bar for Hansel. He devoured it in one quick gulp, and I hoped it would give him enough energy to make it a little farther before we stopped for the night. I wanted to get through this herd of walruses as soon as possible.

When I stood from the ground again, Hansel looked up at me like I was a lunatic.

"I know, buddy," I told him. "I'm tired, too, but we have to get through this cove, and then we can sleep."

He blinked at me. Of course he didn't understand me, but it felt good to talk. It broke up my loneliness and fear. And I had to believe hearing my voice was a comfort to him.

In truth, I had no idea what he was thinking. If there was one thing I was learning from the Arctic, it was that there was a wide gap between me and the wilds of the natural world, a gap that wasn't nearly so big for Hansel. He was a mystery to me, as perhaps I was to him.

That was the magic of the friendship between us, though, the bond we had built through years of training and play. We didn't have to understand each other to need each other. We didn't have to think the same way, or even be the same species to help each other survive.

I slung the backpack onto my back and gave Hansel a "follow me" whistle and sure enough, he popped up onto his front fins and followed right on my heels. With every step, his whole body rocked from side to side, but he kept up with me and I took comfort in the fact that he could probably move a lot faster on land than a big fat walrus could. I picked up the pace as we reached the bend in the ice that turned into the cove.

The sound of the walrus herd became thunderous; the sound of the terns up above was piercing. When I saw the walruses laid out on the U-shaped ice in front of me, I balked.

Hansel, still lunging forward, bumped into my legs and nearly knocked me over, but I kept my balance and we both stood stock-still, staring at the great mass of fur and tusk ahead of us. There were at least four hundred of them between us and the other side of the cove.

Just one male Pacific walrus can weigh around four thousand pounds, with three-foot tusks like double swords hanging from its mouth. A walrus hardly has any fur, but its skin is thick and tough. In the early spring, these large groups of males gather together on the sea ice before heading off to search for mates on the other side of the Bering Strait.

Just like any large group of men stuck together in close quarters — like on a navy ship, for example — they are loud, and stinky, and fights tend to break out suddenly and end just as suddenly. The walruses across the ice were trying to figure out who was in charge, and tusk clashed with tusk, eyes flashed with rage, as in a cacophony of roars and groans, they fought one another for dominance.

I figured they were so busy with one another, they might just ignore Hansel and me. We weren't a threat to them and we weren't their natural food. We were just passing through.

As I watched two particularly menacing bull walruses body-slam each other and bite at each other's faces, Hansel let out a high-pitched bark.

"Yeah," I told him. "I have a bad feeling about this, too." I patted him on the head. "But let's try to keep the barking to a minimum."

He barked again.

"Great," I said. I'd never trained him to shush.

The other side of the U-shaped cove was about sixty yards across the water. The walk around on the ice was maybe three times that. At Hansel's pace, it'd take us half an hour to walk it together, and he'd probably draw the attention of every one of the gargantuan creatures before we made it. I hated to separate, but it was the best option.

I signaled him for his attention, then pointed to the far side of the cove and gave him the signals to go, then to surface, then to wait. At least he knew how to do all those things.

He barked once more, happy to have clear instructions for the first time all day, and then he dove from the ice into the water, his camouflage vest making him almost invisible below the sun-dappled surface.

I set off the long way around, through the herd.

There was a large, flat expanse of ice at the base of the U shape, like a beach of ice, where most of the walruses had congregated. A few of the weaker ones and the big ones who'd lost their fights for dominance were spread out on the edges. The walls of the cove, which shielded it from the cold wind, were no higher than me in some places, but sloped upward in the back to form a great high wall of ice, which allowed no escape, but also prevented any ambush from behind. It would've been a safe and comfortable place to camp out and I understood why this herd had chosen it. I just wished it were a little wider so I didn't have to get so close.

I walked briskly, not fast enough to startle them but definitely not slow, either. I wanted to get this walk over with.

One of the smaller males, perhaps tired from having just lived through his first Arctic winter, lifted his head from the ice as I passed him. He swiveled around like an owl, watching me curiously, and I fought the urge to wave at him and say hello. I spent so much time talking to Hansel, it just seemed natural to greet this little fellow.

Little was a relative term, of course. He probably weighed about 1,600 pounds and was over eight feet long, more than double Hansel's size and not done growing.

I kept my mouth shut and got as close to the ice wall of the cove as possible, trying to slip behind the bulk of the group, who were closer to the water's edge. The older walruses were too busy with each other or with sleeping to pay me any attention. I stepped carefully as I neared the place where most of them were lying, side by side as close as matching socks. I tried to breathe quietly, even though they were so loud that I could have been shouting and they probably wouldn't have heard me.

When I reached the halfway point, where the U shape turned back out toward the other side, the walruses were so crowded on the ice that I had to press my back flat against the high wall to slip by.

Through the noise, I heard Hansel's high-pitched bark, and I looked across the field of brown fur and heaving blubbery chests to see my partner standing on his front flippers at the end of the cove, watching my progress with impatient curiosity.

I knew it wouldn't work, but I looked directly at him and put my gloved index finger to my lips and shushed_ him. I even went, "Shhhhushhh," though there was no way he'd hear me, even with the sea lion's excellent hearing, or if he did hear me, that he'd know what *Shhhhushhh* meant.

He barked again.

And, distracted, my boot stepped right down on the front flipper of a long-tusked, whisker-faced walrus, who yanked it out from under me so fast that I toppled back against the ice and fell. He reared up over me, his entire massive body blocking out the sky. His ivory tusks shimmered, each longer than my forearms, and he roared with a wide-open pink mouth and a blast of stinking air.

I yelled like an idiot, hoping to frighten him off.

My breath must not have been bad enough, though, because he just roared louder. I covered my head with my hands, bracing myself for his two-ton body to crash down on me. I wondered if I'd actually feel his tusks crush my skull or if I'd die of fear first.

At least I had *some* instincts, because even though my mind wondered about dying, my body wanted to live and it made me roll sideways before the walrus landed on top of me. My backpack hit the next walrus, and I used that one's body as leverage to push myself up to my feet again.

My attacker turned his whole neck around and tried to swipe at me with his tusks, which missed and cut into his unfortunate neighbor.

I tried to run backward, but I tripped on another walrus and found myself backed up against the ice again, this time with two angry walruses in front of me, both maneuvering to smash me to bits. I heard Hansel bark and then saw through the sliver of space between their bodies as Hansel jumped from the ice sheet into the water to swim back across for my rescue.

"No, Hansel!" I yelled, but he was already on his way.

It would take a miracle for either of us to get out of this alive, and there was nothing I could do to help him. There was nothing I could do to help myself. I did the only thing I could think to do: I closed my eyes and said a prayer for his safety — for mine, too, or if not, at least, for a painless death.

I didn't expect to hear a response, but nature had its own bloody way of answering my prayers.

I heard a crack and opened my eyes to see the polar bear that had been stalking me crash through the ice, charging into the walrus cove.

He hadn't come to save me. He'd come to snare a meal. But in that moment, his blood-spattered white fur looked to me like salvation.

16:
DEATHMATCH

THE two big walruses in front of me turned their heads as the bear rushed in and cries and growls of alarm went up throughout the herd.

Their distraction gave me enough time to lunge sideways past them and break at a full sprint across the ice, jumping between surprised walruses like I was jumping through the tire obstacles at football practice.

Normally, a polar bear wouldn't try to eat a walrus. They're too large, too powerful, and too dangerous if it came to a struggle. But if he could surprise a herd, he might just get lucky and catch an injured, frail, or sick walrus and eat enough to survive for weeks on his journey from the sea ice to the land where he'd spend the summer. Ever the calculating hunter, the polar bear apparently considered the risk of attacking a walrus herd worth the reward.

The walruses began to jump back into water, where the polar bear wouldn't dare pursue them. Giant masses of blubber and tusk slammed into one another, crashing over one another in a panicked flight from the ice. The water in the cove transformed from a placid bay of Arctic blue into a frothing white whirlpool of ivory and fur and, I noticed . . . blood.

In their frantic escape, some of the walruses had been injured, not by the bear, but by other walruses.

The walruses who'd been attacking me had turned toward the water, too, although they had a long distance to go. The larger of the two knocked the smaller one from his path and thrust his chest forward faster than I had imagined such an animal could move. The other rolled back up onto his front flippers and heaved himself toward the water as well.

And then I saw Hansel, swimming against the herd of walruses, struggling for a path back onto the ice, back to me.

I pointed, urging him to head for clear water, but he was determined, dodging and weaving his lithe body through the crowded ocean. At one point, his small brown face popped up between two walruses, only to vanish beneath them as one rolled and dove beneath the water.

"Hansel!" I yelled. I couldn't help it. I feared he'd been crushed.

But he surfaced again, leaping onto the ice and waddling over to me as if nothing remarkable had happened.

And yet something remarkable was happening at that exact moment.

Two walruses remained on the ice sheet, directly across the water from where I stood.

One, a young pup, had been lying near the spot where the bear had entered the cove and had not moved fast enough to escape or defend himself. The bear had stunned him with one powerful swipe of his massive front paw. The ice ledge was narrow at that point, and the walrus pup had managed to roll partway to the water, sluggish, but trying to escape.

The second walrus, a full-grown bull, had moved to protect the pup, throwing himself forward with his full strength to intercept the bear.

The bear reared back on his hind legs, rising up to nearly ten feet high. The walrus leaned back, using his tail to lift his body so the bear couldn't pounce down on him.

The bear swiped a paw at the walrus as the walrus swung his neck forward, smashing his head and tusks sideways into the bear's chest, even as the bear's claws scratched deep grooves in his skin.

The bear was knocked backward, but spun with a roar and delivered a pistonlike blow straight on with his snout, directly into the walrus's throat. The walrus was knocked back and the bear followed with a thrashing of his claws and then a bite to the throat. Bright red blood drenched his jaws and spurted across the ice. The seal pup had regained his senses in the meantime and, unsentimentally, dove away, vanishing below the water without the slightest move to help the walrus that had saved him.

The walrus wasn't done fighting yet, though.

He heaved his body up and shoved himself hard against the bear's face, forcing the animal to loosen its grip, and then he pulled free, hard, leaving a chunk of blubber in the bear's mouth. The walrus delivered a head butt to the bear's shoulder, and the bear fell back. The walrus reared up to tear the bear open with his tusks, but the bear and I appeared to fight the same way because it used my move. It rolled away.

The walrus missed, and his tusks crashed down into the ice hard enough to crack it. That was when the bear delivered the killing blow, both front paws dropping down onto the walrus's head from above, and then ripping out the back of his neck with a massive tearing bite.

The moment after the kill, the bear looked up at me across the cove, jaws dripping with red gore, and his tiny black eyes met mine.

Neither of us moved. Even Hansel stilled at my side. He pressed against my leg, and I realized that he was, in a way, choosing sides. On one side was the bear, who was the perfect animal for the wild Arctic. He was a lone, patient hunter with loyalty only to his appetites and his survival. And then there was me, clothed and weighed down by a backpack, frail and cold and longing to return to civilization. Hansel wasn't human, but he was born into our world and, in a sense, made by us. He could no more be like the polar bear than I could, and that was why he stood by my side. For Hansel, neither the sea nor the land was his home.

I was.

I don't know how long it was that we stood there regarding the bear from our side of the ice while the bear regarded us from his, but I will never forget the feeling I had.

It was not fear I felt, but exhilaration.

I owed that bear my life, yet I also knew it would just as gladly have eaten me if it hadn't caught a walrus first.

I admired him. The bear was a survivor. There was something awe-inspiring in his determination, in the patience it took to stalk across so many miles to find the herd, and the risk he had taken to attack when he was so outnumbered and so easily could have been killed himself. He was an efficient killer, dangerous and beautiful, even as the world was changing around him. The ice sheet melted and changed each year, his swims to shore grew longer, his hunt for food more challenging. Ships and oil rigs arrived in places they'd never been before. They disrupted his hunting grounds, changed the places he could find his prey. But the bear was not defeated.

The bear endured.

Hansel was exhausted and so was I. We had to find a safe place to rest — somewhere away from this bear and any others that might come to eat whatever was left of the walrus carcass after he'd eaten his fill. I'd read stories of polar bears coming from miles and miles away when they caught the scent of blood on the breeze. They were solitary hunters, but they didn't miss a chance to eat, and a bull walrus had enough meat to go around.

The polar bear returned to his meal, his teeth crunching loudly on bone.

"Let's get out of here, Hansel," I whispered to my sea lion. "I promise, we'll make camp soon."

I gave him the signal to jump back in the water for an easier swim, but the moment he turned toward the water's edge, he scuttled backward and barked several loud, shrill barks.

The bear raised his blood-drenched snout from the walrus's side. Then he backed away from the body, lowering himself onto his chest and sliding backward with his eyes fixed on the water.

Hansel barked again and again and again and again.

"What is —?" I started to ask, when I saw the herd of walruses rushing from the water to leap back onto the ice. Every single one of them.

It was a thousand-ton stampede, and it was heading right for us.

17:
KILLER

THE tusked giants flung themselves onto the ice in twos and threes, scrambling over one another to flee the ocean, heaving their bodies at full speed away from the edge. The bear tried to retreat all the way to the back of the cove, but he didn't make it. Six walruses charged over him, trampling him underneath like he wasn't even there.

More followed, every bit of ice filling with them and their thundering roars. I looked to the water to my right and saw a mountain of fur rising from the emerald-green sea straight for the spot where Hansel and I stood. It was halfway out of the water before my brain could tell my body to react.

We were going to be crushed!

I spun down to a crouch and thrust my whole body into Hansel's side, wrapping him in my arms and tackling him out of the way. We rolled sideways across the ice, the wind knocked out of me when his body flipped on top of mine.

We hadn't rolled far enough out of the way. Another walrus leapt from the water and loomed over us. Its tusks filled my vision as its silhouette blocked out the sky. I was pinned below Hansel and couldn't move.

There was no escape.

The walrus came down on Hansel just as I pushed with every bit of strength I had to roll us one more time. I felt the impact of the tusk hitting Hansel's body. He grunted, but we kept rolling and the walrus kept moving away from us.

We came to a stop at the far edge of the cove, where the slope lowered and the ice curved back to the flat sheet once more. I pushed myself onto my knees and ran my hands over the sea lion's body to find where the tusk had hit him. I imagined deep wounds, geysers of blood, the light fading from his humorous eyes.

But he just stared at me, confused.

My fingers found a tear in the fabric of his vest and a bend in the Kevlar layer underneath, but no wound.

The armor had protected us both. If he hadn't been wearing the vest, that walrus's tusk might have gone right through him and straight into me beneath him.

I looked to where we had just been standing. Five, then six, then seven walruses roared over the spot. Any one of them would have trampled us, armored vest or no. The bear was already a pulpy heap of lifeless red-and-white fur.

And then I looked to the water and saw what had frightened the walruses so much. The shining black-and-white body of an orca, the killer whale, sliced the surface with its large curved dorsal fin in pursuit of prey.

I'd read about orcas in a nature magazine. The name *killer whale* is actually a mistranslation of an old Spanish name for them, *asesina ballenas* — *whale killer* — because they regularly hunt whales. They're intelligent, fast, powerful, and have no natural predators to fear. They are also social animals, traveling and hunting in groups, just like a pod of dolphins. Where there's one killer whale, there are probably more.

Among the Kwakwaka'wakw people, a native people of the Arctic, there were ancient myths about the killer whale as the ruler of the undersea world, who kept dolphins for warriors and sea lions as slaves.

I wrapped my arms around Hansel, holding him tightly as we watched the killer whale hunt.

A walrus cub, perhaps the very one who'd escaped the bear, swam just ahead of it, slightly above it in the water, parallel to the ice, trying to escape.

The cub hit the surface, then corkscrewed its body down to dive, but it was too slow, perhaps still too stunned from the bear's attack or maybe exhausted from the chase. As it turned, the killer whale flicked its tail and twisted its body sideways, dropping its head below the small walrus's body and flicking it up with such force that the walrus cub was tossed a few feet above the surface, then smashed back down into the water with a huge splash.

The orca was waiting for it when it submerged again, and now calmly opened its jaws and snapped them shut around the walrus cub's rib cage. A cloud of blood spread through the water, and the orca dove to devour its prey in the deep.

Hansel and I backed away from the water, from the walrus cove, and from the bloody battle we had just witnessed. His whole body was shaking, probably from stress and exhaustion. Mine was, too.

We had to make camp and rest. I didn't think more polar bears would be coming this way now, not when the walrus herd was back and in such a state of alert, so we didn't need to go so far.

We couldn't go far.

Hansel was too tired to walk on land any real distance, and there was not a chance I'd let him get back in the water, even if he'd wanted to. We made our way on foot away from the brutal cove, back into the flat fields of ice. I was looking for a pressure ridge that would give us some protection from the cold wind and hide the tent from the view of any passing vehicles. I hadn't forgotten that the most dangerous predator in all of the Arctic was still after us: man.

18:
GONE FISHIN'

I SET up my tent and pulled out one of my Meals Ready to Eat, the military-issued ration. I activated the heating element in it, and settled in to a nice warm meal.

Hansel batted his big lashes at me. I figured I had to share.

Before I could offer him some of my food, though, he popped up onto his flippers and waddled away across the ice.

"Where are you going?" I called after him, but then I saw it. Twenty-five yards away, there was a breathing hole. Hansel was dashing over to it.

"Hansel, no!" I called, but he wasn't a dog and he didn't follow commands like that. Without even looking back at me, he slipped into the hole face-first, his tail flippers rising up straight into the sky before he disappeared.

I ran to the edge of the hole and looked down into the dark water. The ice was several feet thick here, and the breathing hole was like a long, wide tunnel, slightly angled so it was harder for a bear waiting above to pounce straight down on a seal coming up to breathe. It was an ingenious design, a reminder of the unique intelligence of a species that had figured out every possible trick to survive up here. I couldn't see anything below.

I reached my arm into the hole, stretching half my body down to slap the surface of the water the way I did in his training pen back in California to call Hansel up to the surface.

He didn't return.

I pulled myself out of the hole again and leaned

back on my heels, resting my arms on my knees in a squat, and I waited. I felt like a polar bear myself, sitting at a breathing hole hoping to catch a sea lion. Except I wasn't trying to eat it, I was trying to protect it.

Minutes passed and my stomach grumbled. I was no longer hungry, but I knew I had to eat, so I went back to my MRE and gobbled it up beside the hole, then packed the trash into my bag again and sealed it so that no bear would pick up the scent and come to investigate.

And then I waited some more.

A sea lion can hold its breath for about fifteen minutes. Any longer and they drown. If Hansel couldn't find this hole again, there was nothing but solid ice in every direction.

I checked my watch. It had been about ten minutes since he went under.

And then twelve.

Thirteen.

And then, I saw movement. Suddenly, Hansel came charging from the depths, breaking the surface with a great splash of water that froze my face when it hit me. He climbed out of the hole and knocked me over, pressing his snout to my face happily. His breath was heavy with fish.

He'd found dinner, although this time, he hadn't brought me any back.

I patted him on the head, told him *okay* so he knew he'd done well, and then, together, we shuffled back over to the tent. He lay down where I told him to, and I climbed inside, wrapped myself in the blanket, and fell asleep before I could even remember to set the alarm on my watch.

Five hours later, I woke again to relieve myself, drink some water, and pack up our camp. I checked the map and my compass heading again, and determined we were close. If we took a straight course across the ice, we might hit the research station in just another day of walking. It'd be hard for Hansel to cover that distance out of the water, but we didn't have a choice.

We'd rest as much as possible, but I decided that we would not make another camp before we got there. It had been over two days out here in the frozen wilderness, and I had no idea what was happening with my team or with Captain Peterson and his crew. I didn't know if a search party had been sent, or if the navy was trying to find out what happened, or if the mercenaries had simply gunned everyone down to cover up their crimes.

I needed to get to some kind of civilization and find out.

When I finally stood and slung my pack on my back, Hansel looked up at me from the ice. He exhaled loudly and snorted at the air. He made no move to stand.

"Come on, pal, it's almost over," I told him, but still, he didn't move. "Listen, we've got to do this. I can't leave you here."

Nothing.

I gave him the signal to follow me, the signal he always obeyed, but he still didn't move.

Had he been hurt? Was he sick?

I bent down to try to examine him for injuries, when, at the same moment, there was a crack, and a shard of ice popped up from the ridge beside me like a popcorn kernel. For a moment, I thought that the ice was breaking up and feared we'd fall through into the ocean below.

Another crack snapped in the cool air, another pop of ice jumped.

And then I saw the snowmobile in the distance and the man behind it, with his rifle resting across the seat, firing at me.

The Nameless One.

Of course it would be him.

I dropped down behind the pressure ridge for cover just as the third shot hit. Luckily, we were far enough away that his shots hadn't been accurate. The first two had probably taught him how the wind was affecting his aim, and the third one might have found my head if I hadn't hit the deck.

The problem was, the ridge provided cover from only one side, and I knew the mercenary was not alone. If the others flanked me, I was totally exposed. I couldn't stay here, but I couldn't get up.

"Come out now, sailor," Nicolás called. "The rest of your crew is safe and warm. Wouldn't you like to join them? Surrender and turn over the data, and you can all go home alive."

I knew he was lying. There was no way he could let me live, no way he would. Especially not now that he knew I'd taken the data.

I heard the engines of a few snowmobiles rev up. They were moving around to take me out. They must have abandoned the large transport truck and switched to the much faster and lighter snowmobiles back at their base.

As they sped around to flank me, I was trapped, like the prey I had just seen feasted upon by the killer whale. If I didn't find a way out, Hansel and I were dead.

I had to think of a way to survive in a landscape that was hostile to the very idea of survival. Humans weren't meant to live up here. We weren't designed for it; we didn't have the right kind of intelligence. But some animals were. Some animals did.

Like the seals, who'd punched that breathing hole in the ice.

I'd spent so long working with Hansel, training him to be around people, to work with us, to play with us, even to wear a vest and salute like us. I'd gotten him to act like a person, but if we were going to live, it was time for me to act like a seal.

I took the emergency oxygen tank from my backpack, shoved one of the chemical heating pads down my shirt, dropped the dynamite and detonator in my pocket with the smoke grenade, and then I pulled out the flare gun.

I fired a shot to distract the mercenaries. A bright red streak flashed toward the blond mercenary, and he dove for cover. At my signal, Hansel and I sprinted together for the breathing hole. I heard more gunfire. The ice around me kicked up as the bullets hit.

I activated the heat pack against my chest, hoping it would keep my body temperature high enough to survive for a few minutes, and then my sea lion and I jumped, disappearing into the Arctic Ocean underneath the ice.

19:
STANDOFF

NEITHER the rush of adrenaline from my mad dash, nor the heat pack pressed against my skin could keep the cold from punching me in the chest. Like before, it felt as if the air had been sucked out of my lungs at the same time as my face ignited in flames.

I pressed the oxygen mask to my mouth and blasted a breath in.

My lungs were full now. I wasn't going to drown right away, although my clothes were beginning to get waterlogged. I was sinking. I kicked furiously, but I was still pulled down. A shaft of sunlight pierced through the breathing hole, but the rest of the surface had a strange dull glow to it, where the thick ice filtered the light. The ocean was dark below my shoes, sinking to depths I couldn't even begin to imagine. Somewhere down there a navy submarine was prowling. Somewhere down there were, perhaps, more killer whales, too. On the ice above were the mercenaries.

Hansel circled anxiously around me as I sank. His wide eyes were all puzzlement. I gave him the signal to push me, like we did in playtime, and then he dove under me and used the end of his snout to shove me back up toward the breathing hole, up toward life.

Together we rose in the lone shaft of sun like performers in the spotlight. When we'd risen back to the hole, I kicked sideways so that I wasn't right below it, and I held on to Hansel for support. I took another breath from the tank. In spite of the heat pads keeping my body temperature up, my fingers had gone numb. I knew I wouldn't be able to keep warm much longer down here and that when I did get out again, I'd have to work fast to stop the hypothermia.

Before I could get out, though, I had to take care of Nicolás and his men.

I grabbed the stick of dynamite from my pocket and wedged it into the underside of the ice, right into a deep gouge that had probably been made by the claws of the seal who'd originally dug the hole. Then I pulled out the smoke grenade. I took one more deep breath from the oxygen tank, cracked the smoke grenade, and tossed it up through the hole.

Bright green smoke clouded the circle of surface water. I counted down from twenty, urging myself to be patient, not to act too soon.

When I felt enough time had passed, I signaled Hansel to get out of the water, and I held on to his tail. His front flippers gave a powerful upward stroke, and we burst through the water in a cloud of green. I shot my hand out to catch the ice, and I rolled up and out.

Just as I'd thought, the mercenaries had moved in to investigate, surrounding the opening. Hansel's leap knocked one of them over, and my roll took out the legs of a second. I swung the small metal cylinder of the oxygen tank sideways with all my strength, and it crashed into his stomach, then I rolled on top of him, pinning his arms down with my knees. I grabbed his gun, ice falling from my hair. I popped up and aimed the gun toward a silhouette on the other side of the breathing hole that I could just make out through the smoke.

"Don't move!" I shouted. My hands were shaking and my voice trembled, but I held the barrel steady.

The form on the other side of the smoke had a pistol raised toward Hansel. The man at my feet groaned in pain, and the man below Hansel was unconscious. He'd probably smacked his head on the ice pretty hard. At best he'd a have a serious concussion. In truth, I didn't care what happened to him.

"My sniper has his sights on you as we speak," the form called to me through the smoke. It was Nicolás. "He can put a bullet through your brain before you can even think to squeeze your trigger. Drop your weapon."

The sniper, however, was on the same side of the green smoke as Nicolás, and at least eight hundred yards away. There was no way he had a clear shot at me, not from so far, over the pressure ridge and through the green smoke. I was sure Nicolás was bluffing.

Well, I was *mostly* sure Nicolás was bluffing.

I glanced to the snowmobile that had been left running just behind me. I started to edge toward it.

"I'm not dropping my weapon until you all drop yours," I said as bravely as I could.

He didn't lower his gun. It was still pointed at Hansel, but no sniper shot came, either. I was still alive.

I could no longer feel the heat packets against my skin, though. I was going numb all over. My clothes were frosted, the water from the ocean freezing in the air while I stood. I needed to get myself out of the wet clothes and get warm. The longer this standoff went on, the less chance I had of surviving it. I hoped Nicolás couldn't see my lips turning blue.

We stood like that for a while. The only sounds were our breathing and the pop, crunch, and crackle of the sea ice reminding us that it wasn't solid ground on which we stood. My teeth stopped chattering, which was a very bad sign. The green smoke started to thin. Any second, Nicolás and the sniper would be able to see me clearly, a half-frozen sailor whose fingers were probably too numb to pull the trigger.

But I had one more trick up my sleeve.

I whistled loudly and Hansel turned toward me, then I pressed the detonator switch and set off the dynamite.

The blast shook the thick ice, knocking Nicolás off his feet. He cried out as he fell and his shoulder hit just on top of the blast site. The newly fragile ice cracked open like an eggshell, and he splashed through it.

Hansel, following my whistle just as he'd been trained, charged on his flippers through the smoke cloud right to my side, startled by the blast, but certain that my whistle was calling him to safety, as it always had. I jumped onto the snowmobile, glad they'd left it running. I'd never actually driven a snowmobile before. It was a day of firsts for me. How hard could it be?

"Hop up," I told Hansel. I tapped the seat behind me, showing him where to go.

Hansel hesitated. Shots tore wildly through the thinning smoke as the Nameless One opened fire at me, even though he couldn't see clearly. Nicolás thrashed and clawed for the surface, trying to get out of the water. I felt bad for him, but I was in trouble myself.

"Hansel, please." I signaled him again to jump on, the same way I signaled him to get onto a boat. He was frightened of the unfamiliar machine, confused by it, but his eyes met mine and he knew, in that animal brain of his, that he could trust me. He climbed awkwardly onto the seat, lying down sideways across it. I felt the weight of the machine shift as the front of the treads lifted from the ice. I leaned forward and opened the throttle.

The engine squealed and strained, but we moved, racing toward the research station on a stolen snowmobile as fast as it could carry us.

20:
DRIVING LESSONS

THE wind bit at my face, but I couldn't feel it. The heat of the engine warmed my thighs, but even so, my vision was narrowing. I forgot I was driving and veered across the ice sideways, then course-corrected and nearly flipped us over. I knew my thoughts were jumbled, I knew hypothermia was setting in, but I didn't stop. I couldn't stop. As soon as Nicolás was out of the water, the mercenaries would come after me.

Maybe they already were after me. Maybe they were ahead of me? Which way was I going?

I couldn't tell. Was that a research station I saw or a mirage, like in the desert? Were there mirages on the ice? Was I dreaming?

I wondered if I could just sleep while I drove, just close my eyes for a second. I was so tired. So very tired. Maybe I could get one of the mercenaries to drive me the rest of the way, while I slept.

What?

These were crazy thoughts I was thinking, the thoughts of someone confused by an extreme state of hypothermia, someone whose blood was leaving his brain.

The mercenaries were my enemy. They were trying to kill me. They wouldn't help me drive.

But Hansel was on my side. Hansel was smart. Hansel would let me sleep.

"Hey, Hansel," I said out loud. "Why don't you drive?"

I guess that was when I passed out and the snow-mobile swerved and crashed, because that's one of the last things I remember, except for the sudden feeling of warm liquid on my face. It tasted metallic.

It was blood.

I also remember looking at Hansel lying beside me, the snowmobile flipped over somewhere behind us, and I remember saying to Hansel, "Wow, buddy, you're a terrible driver," although I knew it was me who'd crashed, me who was passing out, and me who had failed to save us.

I hoped I was tasting my own blood, not his.

My vision went blurry, then it went black.

21:
THE FINNISH LINE

HEARD voices calling me from the light.

"Keene! Keene!"

There was warmth on my face, warmth surrounding me.

I must be in heaven, I thought. *Strange that the angels would use my last name.*

"Keene, can you hear me?"

Strange that the angels would sound just like Bryson from my Marine Mammal team.

The strangeness of that thought pushed me to open my eyes and see that I was very much still alive and that

Bryson was leaning over me, with Dr. Morris and Kincaid standing behind him. There was a light hanging from the ceiling above me. I was lying on a cot, my feet elevated. I had on warm, dry clothes that didn't belong to me and was wrapped in blankets. There was an IV needle in my arm and fluids being administered through a drip.

But I wasn't in a hospital.

"You're in the Finnish research station, Jäälautta 4," Dr. Morris said, reading the confused expression on my face.

"Jäälautta means 'ice raft,'" Bryson told me. "This place is sitting on a twelve-square-mile ice floe. They found you at the edge of it."

"Where is —?" I started to ask.

"Hansel's fine," said Dr. Morris. "He had a few scrapes and was a little malnourished, but when the researchers called us about you, we brought everything he needed. He's safe."

I felt well enough to sit up on my cot. "What happened?"

"The Finns saw a cloud of green smoke in the sky a few miles from here, and they took out snowmobiles to investigate," Dr. Morris said. "That's when they found you and Hansel. You'd been reported missing the day before, so they knew to call us."

"They also found three mercenaries on the ice," Kincaid said.

"Three?" I cocked my head.

"Nicolás fell through," Kincaid explained. "They said he couldn't get out and sank in his gear. Drowned under the ice, they think. Not much hope of finding his body."

"But how did you all get away?"

"They released us after a few phone calls between Moscow and Washington, DC," Captain Peterson said from the doorway. He nodded to me in greeting. "Like I told you, no one wants a shooting war up here."

"So they just let you go? For nothing?"

"The captain made a deal," Bryson said, not even

bothering to hide the disgust in his voice. "He agreed to share the data from our underwater explorations."

I nodded. It figured. The captain was a coward. Or a diplomat. Or both. "The thumb drive was in Hansel's vest," I said.

"We know," the captain said. "Dr. Morris retrieved it for us."

I gave her a look of disapproval, but she shrugged. It wasn't like she had much choice.

"We also agreed," the captain continued, "to forget any *uncomfortable* accusations about what happened up here."

"So they just get away with what they did?" I asked.

The captain nodded. "They paid a high price for it," he said. "It cost a man his life. And two of the others are quite injured."

"They tried to kill me *and* to kill Hansel," I objected.

"The bad guys don't always get their comeuppance in the world," Captain Peterson said. "This isn't a movie. Diplomacy sometimes involves forgiving wrongdoing even when forgiveness isn't exactly deserved. And if we started making accusations about attempted murder, it might interfere with all the other research up here."

"You don't mean research," I said. "You mean oil companies."

He pursed his lips, but didn't argue with me. "The world needs oil." He paused, then cleared his throat. "They have decided to deny that the mercenaries were ever here, as long as we deny that *you* were ever here."

"The navy has classified this entire incident," Dr. Morris explained.

"Let me guess," I said. "They don't want anyone to know they were going to let a bunch of hired goons from a Russian oil company kill a navy sea lion? And I'm just supposed to forget all this and take Hansel back to them like nothing ever happened?"

"Well . . ." said Kincaid, her eyes downcast. "There's more to the deal."

"Hansel?" My voice caught in my throat.

She nodded. Bryson looked away.

The veterinarian shook her head. "The navy has determined that Hansel never existed."

"Excuse me?"

"They made a deal with the Finns who rescued you," she said. "They get access to the undersea data, too. In exchange for taking Hansel."

"Taking him?" I nearly jumped from the cot, but my head swam. I was dizzy and still quite weak. I tried to remove the needle from my arm, but my fingers were clumsy and stung with frostbite.

"They will transport him safely to the Nausicaa Centre National de la Mer in France," Dr. Morris told me. "It's one of the largest aquariums in the world, and they have a sea lion reserve where he'll be quite happy."

"They can't do that," I said. "They can't just . . . give him away."

"He belongs to the United States Navy," Dr. Morris said. "They can do with him as they please. This is the best thing for him, under the circumstances. He'll be able to socialize with other sea lions, to live comfortably and have the best medical care in the world."

"There has to be another way," I said.

"Officially, he no longer exists," Dr. Morris said. "So the only other way would be for him truly not to exist anymore."

I swallowed hard. I knew what that meant.

"But . . ." My head was cloudy. I couldn't find any more words. "Let me see him," I said.

"Rest," Dr. Morris said, patting me on the arm. "You need your rest."

"I need to see him!" I swung my feet to the floor, but Bryson's hand pressed on my chest, pushing me back down onto the cot. He looked worried, but he didn't look at me.

"Why can't I see him?" I demanded. "Why can't I see Hansel?"

"You've been in and out of consciousness for three days." Dr. Morris took my hand in hers. "A transport team from France already took Hansel. This morning. He's on his way to France as we speak."

"But I didn't . . ." I could feel tears welling in my eyes. "I didn't get to say good-bye."

Hot tears streamed down my face, but the heat was only on the surface. Inside, I felt as if my heart had just frozen as solid as the polar ice. I was surrounded by people for the first time in days, but I felt more alone than I ever had in my life.

My sea lion was gone.

EPILOGUE

I was a gorgeous late spring day in the city of Boulogne-sur-Mer on the northwest coast of France. Tourists from all over the world strolled through the narrow streets to gawk at the medieval castle in the center of town and snap selfies with the twelfth-century bell tower behind them.

I had no interest in that kind of thing. I walked briskly for the coast, nearly jogging. I was afraid I'd be late. I'd missed the earlier train from Paris, because my flight out of New York had been delayed. I'd left San Diego two days earlier and only had two more days of leave to get all the way back to my duty station. I had a new sea lion to train, and the earliest days of training were vital to establishing a bond between us. His name was Banjo and he was a quick learner, but I had business to take care of at this aquarium before I could get back to work with him.

I ran through the historic district of the city, jogged past tour buses and parking lots where locals stood at the edge casting fishing lines into the sea. Some of them even sat on the trunks of their cars while they fished. Such was the way of things in a port city. Everyone but me seemed relaxed.

I ignored them all as I came up to the white concrete and shining glass entrance to the Nausicaa, Europe's largest center of aquatic life. Three different security guards had to point me in the direction of the sea lion sanctuary before I finally arrived, breathless and sweaty, at the outdoor arena that wrapped around the sea lion pool.

I took my seat and waited for the show to start.

The trainers in blue shirts came out to the applause of an excited crowd. One by one, they introduced the sea lions, demonstrating tricks and feeding them and explaining all about their lives in the wild and their lives in captivity.

A sea lion they called Luc showed off jumping, while a big male named Francois let a little girl from the audience pat him on the head and then opened his mouth to let her gently brush his teeth.

The crowd burst into applause at that one.

I kept looking over the other sea lions, the ones lazing around on the rock formations, or floating peacefully in the pools.

I didn't see the one I was looking for, and I sat there for the entire feeding and show just waiting. When it was over, I rushed to the front, practically knocking all the little kids there out of my way.

"Sorry, sorry, pardon, *excusez-moi*," I murmured in a mixture of English and the French I could remember from sixth grade.

When I reached the front, I called up to the nearest trainer. "Excuse me? Do you speak English? *Parlez-vous anglais?*"

She smiled at me. "Yes, I do," she said. "You have a question about our California sea lions?"

"Yes. Well . . . I . . ." I rubbed the back of my neck, suddenly at a loss for words. "I'm not sure how to ask this, but . . . I think I know one of your sea lions. I just wanted to say hi to him."

She wrinkled her brow me. I could imagine how crazy I looked, a sweaty American with a buzz cut talking about how I knew a sea lion in her aquarium in France. I'd think I was crazy if I'd been her.

I tried to explain. "He would have gotten here a few months ago from, well, Finland, I guess? Maybe had a few small injuries from . . . I guess I don't know what they told you. They probably didn't tell you what really happened, but I promise, I knew him. I can't say where or how, but he and I . . . we saved each other and I . . . I just . . . I never said good-bye."

She stared at me, her mouth hanging slightly open. I wondered if she was going to call security on me. I wouldn't have been surprised if she had.

Instead, she strolled over to the barrier where I stood and leaned in close to me.

"You are from the navy?" she whispered.

My heart leapt and my face broke into a smile. I nodded eagerly.

"They call him Hannes," she said. "And told us they purchased him from Canada, but we knew. He responds to English commands, not French or Finnish, of course."

"He's . . . he's okay?"

"He's very happy here, I think," she said. "But he had some strange . . . how do you say . . . *habitudes*."

"Strange habits?" I asked.

She gave me a wry smile and lifted a walkie-talkie to her lips. She said something into it that I couldn't understand. Then we waited. She gave me a wink.

All of a sudden, one of the barred doors at the back of the exhibit lifted up, and a big brown sea lion with a tan snout came ambling out. His eyes scanned over the scene in front of him, and when they caught on the nearest trainer, she saluted him. He saluted back, and then she pointed in our direction. She pointed at me.

And he turned.

And he saw me.

And he barked.

Hansel.

Without anyone telling him what to do, my old partner dove, flippers slicing the water, and he shot like a streak of furry lightning to the exhibit edge. He burst from the pool directly in front of me.

My arms wrapped around him over the railing, and he nearly pulled me over into the saltwater tank as his whole neck embraced me, rubbing his snout in my hair. I breathed deep his fish and fur stench, and loved it, though it could probably make a normal person lose their lunch. To me, it was the smell of life.

Hansel didn't bark again and I didn't say a word. We just held on like that, him halfway out of the water and me leaning halfway in, somewhere in between both our worlds. Neither of us were exactly where we belonged, but we were together, at least for a moment, before he sank down, and I let go.

The handlers at the aquarium let me spend the afternoon with him. He showed me new tricks and I gave him fish, and even if we'd never be a team again, I knew he was safe and he would stay safe and he hadn't forgotten me.

I, of course, would never forget him.

We endure.

AUTHOR'S NOTE

ENDURANCE, like the rest of the books in the Tides of War series, is a work of fiction. The United States Navy Marine Mammal Program is a real program and they really do use thirty-five California sea lions in a variety of roles, but there is no such sailor as Ryan Keene, nor any such sea lion as Hansel, and the navy would not, under almost any circumstance I can imagine, allow one of their sea lions to be executed. That was a dramatic device I invented for the story.

I did, however, base much of what Hansel is capable of doing on the very real workings of the Marine

Mammal Program, specifically the MK 5 "QuickFind" System.

Since 1960, the Navy has used marine mammals like dolphins, orcas, beluga and pilot whales, as well as sea lions, in a lot of different ways. They locate equipment on the seafloor, detect and mark undersea mines so that they can be disarmed, and patrol ports to prevent swimmer attacks. They are also used for research, in partnership with universities around the country, to learn more about the unique intelligence and capabilities of these remarkable creatures.

The navy claims the program is being phased out, with many of the dolphins and sea lions to be replaced by underwater robots beginning in 2017, although the program will not be entirely eliminated.

There are five marine mammal systems in the program, which is based in Point Loma, San Diego, under the authority of the Space and Naval Warfare Systems Command. A "system" is an engineering term for a collection of personnel, equipment, processes, procedures, and documentation that all come together to perform a specific job. The five systems in the navy program are called MK 4, MK 5, MK 6, MK 7, and MK 8. Some animals are used in more than one system, depending on the need, and some animals are cross-trained to be used in more than one way, and some systems use both dolphins and sea lions. MK 5, the system I describe in this book, uses only sea lions.

The sea lions in the navy are given the same quality of care as sea lions in aquariums around the country, and the navy follows the same rules and guidelines for their care as any civilian institution, including the Marine Mammal Protection Act (MMPA) and the Animal Welfare Act (AWA). The navy does have a few exemptions from these laws for "national security," but they claim these exemptions do not impact the safety or care of the animals. The uncertainty surrounding these exemptions, however, gave me the room to invent the story you've just read. It might not be true that they would sacrifice the life of a sea lion for the strategic goals of the United States in the Arctic, but it is possible, and that possibility allowed me to create this story.

To learn more about the real Marine Mammal Program, as well as the use and care of its dolphins and sea lions, you can visit the navy's Space and Naval Warfare Systems website at www.public.navy.mil /spawar/Pacific/71500/Pages/default.aspx or check out *Sea Lions in the Navy (America's Animal Soldiers)* by Meish Goldish (Bearport Publishing, 2012), which provides a realistic illustrated look at what the navy's sea lions can do.

Another true-to-life element that I relied on for this story is the Arctic setting itself and the conflicts that are erupting over it. The Arctic ice sheet is as much a character in this book as the humans and animals. It really is melting more and more each year as the climate warms, and this melting has opened up new passageways for shipping, new areas for oil and natural gas exploration, and new conflicts over which country has rights in these new areas. According to a report in *The Economist* magazine, the United States Geological Survey has determined that an eighth of the world's untapped oil and perhaps a quarter of its gas lies underneath the Arctic Ocean.

Already, the Russian military has deployed huge resources to the far north, and Canada, Norway, Denmark, and the United States are not far behind. As our hero notes in the story, there really is a US submarine patrolling beneath the ever-shrinking ice sheet.

As the ice shrinks, life becomes harder for the animals that rely on the ice sheet for hunting, like polar bears and seals. They have to travel farther to find a meal and sometimes go hungry or drown in their wide-ranging quest. These are tough, smart animals, but their lives are being profoundly affected by the changes humans are bringing about in the polar region, and they will have to adapt quickly if they are going to survive.

If you'd like to learn more about the Arctic, its wildlife, exploration on the ice, or the conflicts over it and the changes impacting it, there are a lot of options out there. For more on the conflict over resources as the ice sheet melts, *Arctic Thaw: Climate Change and the Global Race for Energy Resources* by Stephanie Sammartino McPherson (Twenty-First Century Books, 2015) is a compelling introduction that asks a lot of important questions. For a great overview of the animals of the Arctic, DK's Eyewitness series produced the wonderful *Arctic & Antarctic* (DK Publishing, 2012), which is loaded with pictures and descriptions of the animals of the region. There are a lot more books and articles on these subjects, and your school library is a great place to start to your own research.

■　■　■

I would like to thank my editor, Nick Eliopulos, who could not have known the adventures we would go on together when he slipped me a photo of a dolphin and a Navy SEAL and said, "What do you think?" These books have been a joy to create and I cannot thank him enough for giving me the chance. I'm grateful, too, to the rest of the Scholastic team, from David Levithan, who brought me aboard originally, to the talented copy editors who make me seem smarter than I am, and the designers who give these books their signature awesome look. I'm also grateful to the Book Fairs and Book Clubs staff, who work night and day to get the right book to the right kid at the right time. Thanks for sharing Tides of War with so many readers.

I'm also grateful for all the men and women who serve this country in the United States Navy, for the work they do, the skill with which they do it, and the risks so many of them take about which we will never know. While many of their triumphs and their sacrifices remain secret, my admiration need not.

As I've said before, to all the sailors and SEALs out there, as well as the civilians who work alongside them: Hooyah!

COME IN FROM THE COLD . . .

And discover another chilling military
adventure by C. Alexander London!

Read on for a sample of
Dog Tags #3: Prisoners of War.

"**H**ey, Rivera," Goldsmith whispered in my ear. His breath frosted the air between us. "Looks like some kind of fairy tale out there in the woods, don't it?"

Crunchy snow clung to the tree trunks like white fur. I pressed my fingers against the ground in front of me and the snow crackled. I stood up to my shoulders in the icy foxhole. Goldsmith stood beside me, shivering and talking too much.

"I feel like Little Red Riding Hood's gonna come through the forest any second." He laughed. "Off to grandmother's house she goes. Except, she ain't finding no grandmother out here. Just us, the GIs of the Ninety-Ninth Infantry!" He slapped the snow in front of him and laughed again.

I grunted. I didn't think we were supposed to be talking. We were supposed to be watching the forest for Krauts — I mean Germans, German soldiers, Hitler's army. Everyone said the Germans were as beaten as the St. Louis Browns in the World Series, that the war in Europe was about over. Everyone said we'd be home by Christmas.

I didn't want to be home by Christmas. I had just gotten here and I wanted to fight the Nazis, not sit in a frozen foxhole with some guy jabbering in my ear all morning. I kept my eyes fixed on the woods in front of me. The snow wasn't so thick. I could see branches and a few scraggly bushes poking up from the ground, covered in frost, like icing on a cake.

I doubted I'd see anything more exciting than that. They sent the new guys, replacement soldiers like me, out here to the Ardennes forest in Belgium precisely because it had been so quiet. There was little risk that my lack of experience would mess anything up or get anyone killed here.

I couldn't feel my feet in my boots anymore. I hoped they were still there below me. I kicked them against the frozen dirt just to be sure. They stung.

"Hey, Rivera," Goldsmith pressed me. "You hearing me? Do you speak English, even? Huh? You *habla inglés?*"

I rolled my eyes and tried to ignore him.

Goldsmith's rifle lay between us, propped up against the edge of the foxhole, next to my medic's bag. I knew that if he had to use his rifle, I'd probably have to use my medic's bag. I'd had just a few weeks of first-aid training before the Ninety-Ninth Infantry called me up and dropped me down here on the front lines as a replacement soldier the previous night. I didn't even know what unit I was in. A sergeant had simply put me in this foxhole next to Goldsmith in the pitch-black and told us to look out for Germans.

"What we do if they show up, Sarge?" Goldsmith had asked.

"Shoot them," the sergeant grumbled, and stalked away into the cold night.

Goldsmith probably knew as much about fighting the Nazis as I knew about being a medic in a war, but we were stuck together in the foxhole all night, so we both did our jobs and looked out for Germans. I kind of wished I had a rifle instead of a bunch of bandages and a big red cross on my arm.

In boot camp, all the guys had made fun of me for training to be a medic instead of a rifleman, but it wasn't my fault. I *wanted* to fight Nazis. That's why I joined the army in the first place, to show that I was a fighter, that I could be heroic, but the army didn't ask what I wanted when they gave me my assignment.

I scanned the dim forest, shivering through my thin coat, but I didn't see anything to make me worry. Somewhere in the night a heavy artillery barrage cut loose. A lot of firepower. The ground vibrated beneath us, even though the attack was miles away.

I figured it was our guys, way down the front line — but how far, I couldn't tell. I figured I wouldn't want to be the Germans fielding those incoming shells. I almost felt bad for them. Except they were Nazis, so I figured they were getting what was coming to them.

I hugged myself and rubbed my shoulders to keep warm. My fingers squeezed the checkerboard patch on my shoulder, the insignia of our division. The Ninety-Ninth. They called us the Battle Babies because by 1944, we still hadn't seen real combat. There had been some fighting a few days back, while I was still in France on my way to the front. I was disappointed to miss it. It was bad enough to be in the war without a weapon, but if I never got the chance to be in a battle, how would I ever hold my head up high back home? It felt like high school baseball all over again. I rode the bench in baseball, and now I was riding the bench in the Second World War.

"Rivera!" Goldsmith whisper-shouted at me, fed up with my silence. "I asked if you speak English."

"Yes!" I snapped at him. "I speak English."

"You ain't said a word all night. I thought you might only speak, what? Spanish?"

"I do speak Spanish," I told him. "And English."

"You Puerto Rican?"

"American."

"We're all American . . . but where you from *before* America?"

"I was born in America," I told him.

"You know what I mean."

"My parents are Mexican," I told him, and looked away. I didn't want to see his face. There'd been riots last year all over the country and a lot of people blamed the Mexicans for them. I didn't have anything to do with that stuff, but some people still just didn't trust anyone who spoke Spanish.

But I *was* American, through and through. Why else would I be freezing my behind off in a foxhole in Europe? "I'm from Albuquerque."

"I'm from New York," Goldsmith said. "We got a lot of Puerto Ricans."

I didn't feel like explaining how Puerto Ricans and Mexicans were totally different, so I just shrugged.

"My family's from Lithuania," he continued. "Eastern Europe, you know?"

"Uh-huh," I said, although I wasn't sure what the question was. Goldsmith loved to talk. I was happy to just keep quiet in the early morning light and watch the forest, but he was determined to have a conversation.

"They got chased out for being Jews," he said. "Their homes and businesses burned down, even their synagogue. So they came to New York. Started over. Garment business, right? I guess you figured that."

"Uh-huh," I said again. What did *I* know about New York or Jews or the garment business? I grew up in Albuquerque, New Mexico, played ball in high school, and signed up for the army before I even graduated. I didn't figure anything about anything, except that I was going to fight for my country and I was the only guy in my class going so soon. Other guys in school were bigger and stronger and tougher than me, but they all just sat around waiting for the draft, or waiting for the war to be over. Not me. I didn't wait. I even lied about being eighteen so that I could enlist. I wouldn't be eighteen for another two months, but with Hitler losing the fight, I didn't think I could wait. If the war ended before I got in it, I'd never be able to show just how tough I could be.

"You don't say much, huh?" Goldsmith shook his head.

"Not much to say," I told him.

"You got a problem with me being Jewish?"

That took me by surprise. As far as I knew, I'd never met a Jewish guy before. Was I *supposed* to have a problem with him being Jewish?

"I don't have a problem with that," I told him. "You got a problem with me being Mexican?"

"You said you were American." He smirked. That broke the tension. We both laughed a little. I guess each of us was used to people having a problem with who we were. Now that we were together in this frozen little foxhole in this frozen forest, ordered here by the Ninety-Ninth Infantry Division of the United States Army, the only people we had a problem with were the Nazis.

And we were here to kick their butts all the way back to Berlin.

"Check it out." Goldsmith reached under his shirt and pulled out his dog tags hanging on a chain around his neck. Stamped into the thin metal was his name and the serial number the army had given him, and then the letter *H*.

"For *Hebrew*," he said. "So, you know, if something happens to me they know what kind of prayers to say and stuff."

I nodded. I didn't like to think much about that kind of thing, but I knew it was there. That's part of the medic's job. In case a guy we were treating . . . well. I had a *C* on mine, for *Catholic*. If anything happened to me, they'd call a priest. I didn't know who a Hebrew guy would want called. The woods were so quiet, I didn't figure it would come to that.

"When we get to Berlin, I can't wait to show this to those Nazis." He laughed. "The Nazis think we Jews are nothin'. They think they can just kick us around, bully us, but I'll show 'em. They'll know it was a Jew who beat them."

"I thought you said we were all American?" I cracked a smile at him.

"I'm a New Yorker," he said, laughing. "We're something else all together. Nobody kicks us around. We'll teach Hitler what's what. You and me!"

I nodded. We fell back into a comfortable silence, the chattering of our teeth the only sound I could hear. The sun was just starting to rise. After a few minutes, I guess the quiet got unbearable for Goldsmith, because he started up the whispering again.

"You even know the Little Red Riding Hood story?" he asked me. "I mean, do they have fairy tales in Mexico?"

"Albuquerque's in New Mexico," I said. "And yes, we have fairy tales."

"Your *abuela* tell them to you?" He smirked. *Abuela*. Grandmother. I guess Goldsmith knew some Spanish. "Like I said," he explained. "We got a lot of Puerto Ricans in New York. I picked up a few things."

"Mi abuela me dijo un montón de cuentos," I tried, but he just stared back at me blankly. Guess he didn't pick up *that* much Spanish from his Puerto Rican friends. "Yeah," I told him in English. "My grandmother told me a lot of stories, but they were different from Little Red Riding Hood. Old ones from the little village where she grew up."

"Hey, we got that in common." Goldsmith smiled. "My grandma told me old ones too, from her little village. She only speaks Yiddish, so I never really understood much of what she said."

"What's Yiddish?"

"It's an old Jewish language," he said. "You never heard of Yiddish?"

"No," I said.

I don't know why, but it felt kind of good to be in this frozen little foxhole with another guy whose grandmother spoke to him in a different language. It made me feel less like I was different from all the other guys. At basic training, nobody else spoke Spanish or talked about old folk tales or missed the tamales their grandmothers made.

The thought of fresh tamales made my mouth water. Army food wasn't good, and out here on the front, there wasn't much of it. I was already hungry.

I wanted to ask Goldsmith what kinds of food his grandmother made for him, but he asked me a question first.

"So, down in *New* Mexico, you got snow like this?"

"Nothing like this," I told him.

"You live in, what, the desert?"

"It's not really the —"

He didn't let me finish.

"I guess it don't snow much in the desert," he chuckled. "You know my people originally came from the desert. The Hebrews. Spent forty years wandering in the desert in ancient times. Must have been awful, but at least there wasn't all this snow, right? I'm freezing my schnoz off."

I just wrinkled my forehead at him. I didn't want to be rude, but I couldn't really follow what he was talking about.

"*Schnoz* means nose in Yiddish," he said. "Like Jimmy Durante, the Great Schnozzola?"

I shrugged. I knew Jimmy Durante was some kind of performer, but I followed baseball, not singing and dancing.

"Oy, *boychick*, we gotta give you some culture." Goldsmith shook his head and rolled his eyes at the sky.

"What's *boychick*?" I asked.

"It's like saying *kid*," he explained.

"Like *vato* in Spanish?" I asked.

"*Vato*?"

"Just, like, a guy, a pal," I said.

"*Vaaa-to, va-to, va-va-va-vato.*" Goldsmith played the word around in his mouth, stretched it, rolled it around. I guess we had something else in common aside from our grandmothers and their old stories. We both liked languages.

"So, *vato*," he asked. "You wanna learn some Yiddish?"

The morning was pretty boring so far, so I told him sure I would. Maybe learning a few new words would pass the time. Now that we were talking, I realized it was definitely better than sitting in freezing silence, waiting for something to happen.

"Ok, I guess *yutz* is as good a place as any to start," Goldsmith said.

"What's it mean?"

"A *yutz* is like a fool," he explained. "Like us!" He laughed and slapped at the icy ground in front of him. "Standing in this cold foxhole all night because some generals say we got to. Or, like Hitler, thinking he can beat the whole world in a fight. He's a *yutz* and a half."

"*Yutz,*" I repeated to myself. It was a fun word, felt good in the mouth, even though it was, I guess, kind of an insult.

"So you got some more Yiddish you can teach me?" I asked. "I can't just go around calling everyone *yutz* all the time. I don't want to get —"

"Shh!" He cut me off and grabbed his rifle. He ducked low. I ducked down beside him, so just our eyes and the barrel of his rifle poked above the top of our foxhole. We listened to the forest.

I couldn't hear anything at first. Then there was a loud slap, like a book dropped onto the floor in a silent study hall, and then a whistle in the sky.

"Incoming! Take cover!" someone shouted from another foxhole down the line. I hadn't even known there were any other foxholes up there with us. When I leaned up to try to see who had shouted, Goldsmith yanked me back down just in time for the ground in front of us to explode.

Then another slap, a whistle, and another explosion.

A tree above us burst into flames and smoke, branches crashed onto the crunchy snow of the forest floor. Goldsmith jumped up and raised his rifle. My ears were still ringing and I stayed at the back of the foxhole for a second, kind of in shock. If Goldsmith hadn't pulled me down, I would have died.

He had just saved my life.

"Thanks!" I yelled, but he didn't hear me over the crack of his rifle and the whistle of the artillery.

The Germans were attacking.

WHAT HAPPENS WHEN MAN'S BEST FRIEND GOES TO WAR?

IN AFGHANISTAN...

IN VIETNAM...

IN WORLD WAR II...

IN THE CIVIL WAR...

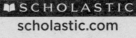

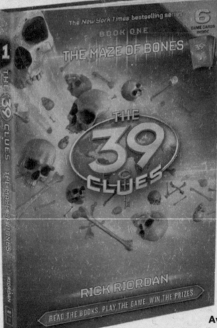